The Weirdness of Willow Street
The Talent Show ©

Written by Danielle Williamson and Tracey Vizzini

For more information, all written inquiries may be sent to:
Wildflowers23@hotmail.com
Traceygiggals@gmail.com

FIRST EDITION

Print ISBN# 978-1-54398-499-6
eBook ISBN# 978-1-54398-500-9

ACKNOWLEDGEMENTS

Thank you to our families and friends that have supported us through this endeavor. We thank you.

Thank you to Lauren Zielenski, Erika Rogers, Denise June McNellis, and Eileen Judge Harvey for their expertise and guidance. We thank you.

A special thanks to our dear friend Pete Flynn for his inspiration and encouragement. We thank you.

Another thank you to Donalen Bowers for her amazing talent that was able to capture our vision. We thank you.

Lastly, a special thank you to our motivator from the spirit realm who guided us through this process. We thank you.

This book is dedicated to our children:
Julian, Leah and Seth

And to all the children around the world.
Always believe!

The Weirdness of Willow Street
The Talent Show ©

Written by Danielle Williamson and Tracey Vizzini

TABLE OF CONTENTS

PART I
Willow Street

CHAPTER 1
The Flyer

PETE LOOKED AT THE CLOCK ANXIOUSLY, AS MR. JACOBS droned on and on about some dude who did something in history. Pete was barely able to focus on anything, except the flyer in front of him. He glanced down at it, and read it to himself again, "Adams Middle School Annual Talent Show. All students welcome. Grand prize: $50.00 and a trophy. Final signup date is May 15th." He looked up at the clock and thought to himself, "Five minutes to go." He quickly began to recall the conversation he had with Alyce and Lily over lunch yesterday.

He had joined Lily at their usual lunch table and handed her another note before he sat down. "I'm not your delivery guy, Lily. You girls are driving me crazy! What is this important document I have been transporting around all day?" he asked sarcastically with a smirk.

"It's just a note with a list of people who are coming to the dance," Lily responded smiling.

"The only notes that I want to be involved with are my music notes, because you do realize we've done nothing, absolutely nothing for the talent show?" Pete expressed with genuine concern.

"I know," Lily responded. "I don't have much either. I haven't been feeling very inspired lately. I need some new sights to sketch."

"Well, I've got to write a song that ties the entire piece together," Pete replied, as he remembered that entering the talent show was his idea. "Maybe I should have entered it alone, that would have been a whole lot easier," he thought to himself.

Now he had to rely on Alyce's photos and Lily's sketches, before he could create the music piece for the talent show. Lily read the flyer over, nervously looked at Pete, and asked, "You did sign us up, right?"

Pete's blue eyes widened, and he nervously ran his fingers through his spiked hair, as he turned to face Lily.

"You mean to tell me, you didn't register us?" he almost shouted at her. The cafeteria got quiet for a second, and everyone turned and looked at them.

"First of all, sit down. You're making a scene," Lily said, glaring back at him.

"I have every right to be upset! I've been working on my music since the day the talent show was announced," Pete replied, beginning to raise his voice louder.

"Well, you should have made a point of registering for it then," Lily hissed back at him.

Pete sat back down and refused to even glance at Lily, as he muttered under his breath, "Everything gets left up to me. Sure, blame me."

Lily looked at him and motioned for him to "Shhhh" with her finger.

"You should know better than to leave something this important up to the two of them." Pete mumbled under his breath.

He met Alyce and Lily the first day of second grade, and he should have known, even then, that they were trouble. Pete's parents had accepted a missionary project that would keep them overseas for several years. They didn't want to move Pete around from school to school, so he moved in with his aunt. Over the years, the girls had gotten them into quite a few sticky situations in the neighborhood. "It's a good thing they have me to get them out of trouble," he thought to himself.

Alyce walked up to the table and could immediately feel the tension between Pete and Lily.

She jumped into her usual seat, pulled her brown hair back into a pony tail, pushed her glasses back on top of her head, and asked, "Okay, what did I miss?" Pete and Lily looked at each other and then at Alyce. They both started talking loudly about what had happened. Alyce let the two of them go on for a few seconds before answering. "Alright, alright, enough you two relax. I registered us for the talent show first thing this morning," Alyce said as she stood up.

"Why didn't you tell us?" Pete asked loudly.

"Number one, it's the first time I'm seeing you all day. Number two, I wanted to see if either one of you would have thought of it, and as usual, neither of you had. I checked this morning and put us on the list, you space cadets," Alyce replied. As Lily and Pete each breathed a sigh of relief, Alyce giggled to herself.

Pete was jolted out of his replay of yesterday's lunch by the last bell ringing. He jumped up, grabbed his books, and joined the other students that were exiting the classroom. He tried to push his way through, saying, "Excuse me. Sorry. I got to go." As soon as he got through the bottle neck at the classroom door, he turned right and headed directly to his locker, weaving in and out of the crowds gathering in the hallway. His friend tried to stop him to ask about their homework assignment, but Pete rushed by him and shouted back, "Sorry, Steve. Not a good time."

Pete finally reached his locker, opened it, and threw his books up on the shelf. He grabbed his guitar, put the strap on, and swung it around his back. He pulled his music sheets out of a notebook and slammed the door shut. He looked up and down the hall and thought "Where are they?" as he paced back and forth in front of his locker, looking at the clock above the auditorium doors. "Sure," he thought, "it's not like we have anything important to do." He turned and saw them slowly approaching, talking and walking with their friends, Denise and Debbie. They were giggling and being silly. As the four girls approached Pete, the conversation quieted down, and Pete rolled his eyes. He couldn't care less what they were gossiping about.

"Hey Pete," Lily said, "Everyone is going to the dance Sunday night. Do you think..." Lily was in the middle of asking, when Pete rudely interrupted.

"That's great, Lily, but we have to go. We've got a lot of work to do," he replied anxiously.

"I hope you two," Pete said, as he motioned towards Denise and Debbie, "have a good time. Alyce, Lily and I have a previous engagement."

"That's not fair," Lily complained and stomped her tiny foot on the ground.

"Sorry, but no. We've got work to do. Besides, we really need to take advantage of the long weekend," Pete sternly said.

Alyce and Lily said "goodbye" to their friends and put their books in their lockers. The three friends headed for the door and bounded down the steps to the sidewalk. Lily looked up at the building and saluted, "See ya Tuesday, Adams Middle School."

Alyce smiled widely, but Pete still looked very serious and distracted. Alyce grabbed him by the arm and said, "Let's go, Cranky," as Lily tagged along behind them, carrying her backpack and humming to herself.

CHAPTER 2

The Neighbors

As they walked the few blocks home, Pete kept rambling on and on about how they had to get right to work, and how they had to work all weekend, with barely a break to eat or sleep. He began to walk faster, and Alyce lagged behind so that Lily could catch up. Once Lily had reached Alyce, she nodded towards Mr. Mason's house and said, "3:30 on the dot." Alyce giggled as they continued to walk.

Mr. Mason was an interesting character. He has been living on Willow Street for his entire life and knew everything about everyone on the street. He is the unofficial "block leader", who planned all the neighborhood parties in the summer. He was a nice enough man, but no one had seen him out of his bathrobe and in regular clothes ever. He even attended the block parties in his short, red satin robe. He mowed the lawn, pruned the hedges, got his newspaper and mail, put out his garbage, and sat on his front porch in his robe! Summer or winter, he was always in a robe. In the summer, he wore a red satin robe with matching flip flops. In the winter, he wore a long, red velvet robe with fuzzy slippers. Today was no different. Mr. Mason smiled and waved at the girls, as he walked to his mailbox in his usual attire. He looked down and said, "Better tie your shoe before you trip," pointing at Alyce's sneaker.

"Thanks, Mr. Mason," Alyce replied. She put her books down on the sidewalk and bent down to tie her shoe.

As Lily waited for Alyce, she looked down the street and noticed her mom's car backing out of her driveway. "Meet me by my house," Lily said to Alyce, as she ran ahead to catch her before she pulled away. "Hey, Mom, wait," Lily yelled ahead. Her mom looked over, stopped the car, and waited for Lily.

"Sorry Lil's I have to go back to work. I know you'll be practicing at Pete's, so I asked Bonnie to look after your brother for the night," her mom said.

"I hope you told her that my room is off limits!" Lily said sternly.

"Yes, I told Bonnie that Lester was not to go anywhere near your room," her mom said smiling.

"Hi, Mrs. Hudson," Alyce said, joining Lily and her mom.

"I've told you a million times, Alyce, to please just call me Joyce," she answered.

Alyce just smiled shyly at her. Her mom's face turned serious and she reached out of the window and grabbed Lily's hand and said, "Listen kiddo, your dad called, he won't be able to make the show." Her mom paused before continuing, "I know you're disappointed Lil, I'm sorry." she said.

"No, it's all right," Lily said sadly looking at the ground.

"I have to run or I'm going to be late," her mom said blowing her a kiss "See you tomorrow. Have fun rehearsing, I love you." and she was on her way.

"I'm sorry, Lily," Alyce said as she put her arm around her and gave her a squeeze. "I know you're sad that your dad is not coming."

"Thank you Alyce, but I'm getting used to it," Lily said as they continued walking towards Pete's house.

Across the street, Mr. Venter was washing his car for the fourth time this week, even though they were predicting rain for most of the weekend. "This guy is going to wash the paint right off his car if he keeps it up," Lily whispered to Alyce as they got closer.

"I think he's just a clean freak," Alyce said "But the green clothes, what's with that?" Alyce asked. Lily shrugged her shoulders.

"You don't think it's strange that everything Mrs. Venter hangs on the clothesline is green? Green sheets, green towels, green socks and underwear. It's the strangest thing I've ever seen, because every time you see them, they're not wearing green," Alyce went on looking at Lily.

Alyce contemplated this for a second, just shrugged her shoulders, and said, "More weirdness on Willow Street."

Alyce looked ahead and saw that Pete had already crossed the street and was approaching his front porch.

"Breathe it in, Alyce, the last few minutes of freedom," Lily said as she looked up at Alyce and laughed.

Alyce giggled, then got serious, and said, "Ok, Lily, we did sign up for this, and Pete is counting on us. Let's try to keep the comments to a minimum and work together to get this done. Maybe we can enjoy a part of the long weekend, if we finish early." Lily looked down and kicked a little pebble down the street.

"Ok, I'll behave," Lily said looking up at Alyce. The two girls looked at each other and burst out laughing.

"Yeah, sure you will, Lil," Alyce said, and they continued to walk the half block to Pete's house in silence.

They were about to pass the house that was owned by the Amatoli's, who were a weird family. They moved in a few years ago, kept the blinds drawn all the time, and kept to themselves. People used to hear strange noises and chanting coming from the backyard. All the neighbors kept their distance.

One day last September, when they were walking home from school, they noticed that the house appeared to be empty. The little girl that lived there was not in school anymore either. No one had seen anyone coming or going for a few days. Finally, after a week, Mr. Mason called the police to come to check on the house and the family.

The police found nothing! The family was gone! Their cars were in the garages. All their keys and phones and other personal items were all there, but they were just gone. They had disappeared into thin air. Some suggested they went on vacation; others gossiped that they were spies or something like that. Mr. Anderson, Alyce's dad, who was a local attorney, tried with no luck to get information on their disappearance. The neighbors constantly asked questions for months, since Alyce and her family lived right next door. It had been about nine months now, and no one ever came to that house. No deliveries, no mail, no newspapers…. until today that is.

Alyce sped up her step and reached the Amatoli's driveway in a split second and glanced down at the magazine laying in the driveway. Lily ran to catch up.

"What do you think of this?" Alyce questioned as she picked up the magazine.

"It's just some advertisement or something," Lily said, as she joined Alyce on the driveway.

Alyce checked the mailing address, and it was correct. She turned the magazine over and read the title, "Unusual Destinations." Alyce looked at the magazine and then up at the house. She had no time to think about this right now and stuck it in Lily's backpack.

"Don't put that trash in my bag!' Lily exclaimed.

"Hey, you never know, maybe there will be something in there that will inspire us," Alyce said with a smile, glancing back at the Amatoli house.

Alyce lived next door to the Amatoli's house her entire life. She lived with her parents and her sister Bonnie and she had always been suspicious of them. So, it didn't surprise her one bit when they went missing. She chalked it up to just being more weirdness on Willow Street.

CHAPTER 3
Off to Work

THEY CROSSED THE STREET AND HEADED DOWN THE STONE path that led to Pete's front porch.

"It's about time!" Pete said as he swung the porch screen door open.

Lily looked down at her wrist, as if she were wearing a watch, and said sarcastically, "Gee, Pete, we got here about thirty seconds after you. We missed SO much. Besides, we would have been here sooner if Alyce didn't stop to pick up trash out of the Amatoli's driveway."

Alyce pinched Lily's arm, as they walked into Pete's house. "Ouch!" Lily squealed, "Okay, Pete, sorry. We're here now, so let's get to work." she said as she rubbed her arm, looking angrily at Alyce.

Pete looked at them suspiciously and said, "Alright, let's go, guys. Straight upstairs."

"Can we at least say 'Hello' to your aunt?" Lily asked Pete.

"Nope, nope, nope." I already told her you said, "Hi." Now get upstairs," Pete said.

"Your aunt is so cool. We shouldn't be rude," Alyce said.

"And she always has fresh baked cookies," Lily added excitedly.

Pete looked at the girls sternly and nodded for them to go upstairs. When they reached the top of the landing, Pete pointed to the door to his room.

"I'm going. I'm going." Lily replied.

Pete opened the door to his room, and the girls walked inside. Lily immediately ran over to Pete's pet cockatoo, Ozzie, and began talking to him. He didn't say much, but Lily was trying to teach him a few words. Pete just shook his head. "Alyce, set an alarm on your phone for two hours, so we can see how much progress we make," Pete said, as he picked up his guitar and adjusted the strap around his neck. He pulled his most recent music sheets out and nodded towards the girls. "Are you girls good? Do you need anything?" he asked. The girls shook their heads. "No? Good, then get to work," he said.

Lily sat on the bed and took her sketchbook out of her backpack. Alyce sat on the floor and began to go through the photos on her camera.

"Lily, can you please hand me that magazine in your backpack?" Alyce asked.

Lily fished around inside the bag and pulled out the magazine. She reread the title "Unusual Destinations" "Weird magazine for weird people," Lily thought as she shook her head and tossed the magazine to Alyce.

Pete sat on his stool and started making changes to the chords he had previously written down on his music sheets. He began chewing on his pencil again when he realized he had absolutely nothing. Nothing! Brick wall. Stumped.

Lily laid on the bed and looked up at the ceiling. "This room is pretty cool, Pete." she said.

"Now you think my room is pretty cool?" Pete answered sarcastically.

"I never noticed the stars and planets on the ceiling either. Do they glow in the dark?" Alyce asked looking up.

Lily jumped up, switched off the lights, and started looking up at the ceiling. She walked back, flopped onto the bed, rolled onto her back to get a better view of the glowing stars, and shouted, "I see the Big Dipper."

"Would you two knock it off already! We're not even here five minutes, and you're already goofing off," Pete said angrily. He crossed the room and turned the light back on.

As he was about to sit back down on his stool, he heard his aunt calling for him from downstairs, "For Pete's sake. What now?" Pete said, loudly slapping his side.

Out of the blue, Ozzie blurted out, "Pete stinks."

"Now you're going to start with me too, Ozzie?" Pete asked.

Lily rolled around on the bed, laughing so hard that she almost fell off. Alyce sat up and held back a giggle, because she saw that Pete was getting furious. Pete left the room in a huff to see what his aunt wanted.

Moments later, Pete walked back up the stairs, loudly saying, "All right, chatterboxes, back to work." Pete was beginning to get a little anxious as he thought to himself, "We only have three days. That is 72 hours to create and complete our collaboration for the show." This was a major undertaking, and the pressure was building! He wanted to get the ball rolling and get this project off the ground.

Pete slowly pushed the door open. He could not believe the site in front of him. Alyce was still laying on the floor, flipping through some crazy looking magazine, and twirling her hair. Lily was sitting on his dresser trying on lip gloss, puckering her lips, admiring herself in his mirror. Pete saw that she had dumped the contents of her backpack onto his bed. The two of them were yapping away about the stupid dance, so engrossed in their gossip that they didn't even realize he had returned. He was furious. He slammed the door closed and shouted, "You've got to be kidding me? I am gone five minutes, and the two of you are already acting up."

Lily was so startled that she jumped off the dresser onto the floor and just looked at him. Alyce had been admiring a beautiful photo in the magazine, when she looked up annoyed and said, "You don't have to shout Pete, we're right here."

He narrowed his eyes and glanced back and forth at them and inhaled a deep breath. He crossed the room and picked up the flyer from his dresser and waved it in the air asking, "Hello? Do you remember this? You know the talent show we signed up for? The one we committed to perform at in three days? I'm really disappointed with the two of you." he continued shaking his head, "I don't appreciate the lackadaisical attitude I am getting."

"Oh Brother, stop being so dramatic. You're a guitar player not an actor," Lily answered sarcastically.

"Besides, this was all your idea," Alyce reminded him with a stern look.

He closed his eyes and took a deep breath, and said more calmly, "I don't feel like you guys are taking this seriously. I leave you for five minutes and you're goofing off. We only have three days and we haven't done a thing and..."

"Ok, ok, we get it, but you need to relax, Pete," Alyce said, cutting him off and continuing, "We're going to get it done." Pete looked at her and shrugged his shoulders.

"Lighten up, DUDE!" "Don't be so serious. This is supposed to be fun," Lily said trying to remind him.

Pete smirked and turned his head towards them and said, "Alright, alright, I'll try to relax, but seriously we need to get back to work."

"You got it," the girls replied, shaking their heads in agreement.

The friends were ready to get back to work. Alyce remained sprawled on the floor and curiously studied the photographs in the magazine. Lily hopped back onto the bed and opened her sketchpad. She sat cross legged and began to draw. Pete went and sat down on his stool and started to tune his guitar. He went to make some notes and his pencil point snapped. "Oh great, what else could go wrong?" Pete thought.

Alyce stopped what she was doing and looked at him and said, "What is it?"

"This isn't a good sign, I broke the point on my last pencil," Pete said holding it up.

Lily grabbed her bag from his bed and tossed it to Pete without even looking up and said, "I should have a pencil somewhere in there."

Pete began to fish around, looking for a pencil. "Are you sure there is one in here?" he asked, as he rummaged through her bag.

"Yeah. Yeah, it's in there," Lily answered absentmindedly.

He began to remove the odd items from her bag, holding each thing up to examine. "She has some weird stuff in here," Pete thought to himself, as he dropped it to the floor. A moment later, Pete finally found the pencil he was searching for. He put her bag on the floor and picked up where he left off.

They worked for some time uninteruppted. Pete huffed in dismay and looked at the girls.

"What's wrong now?" Lily asked looking up at Pete.

"Why don't you play us what you have so far Pete?" Alyce asked encouragingly.

"Great," Pete said under his breath. "Put me on the spot, why don't you?"

Alyce pushed the magazine aside, making room for Lily to join her on the floor. Once they were settled and quiet, Pete began to play the first few notes of the song and stopped. He hung his head and shamefully said, "I don't know why, but I'm stuck. That's as far as I get."

"Try playing that chord three times in a row, maybe a little slower," Lily softly said.

"Yeah, try it Pete," Alyce said in agreement, trying to encourage him.

Pete started over this time, slower and repeating the chord several times in a row. "That's it!" squealed Lily. "Keep going!!" He glanced down at Alyce. She smiled and nodded, as he continued to play, adding another note or two to the song he was writing.

While he played, Alyce looked down at the photo in the magazine. It looked a bit blurry. She rubbed her eyes and put her glasses on, and the picture got even blurrier. She sat up, poked Lily on the leg, and motioned for her to look at the picture. Lily glanced down at the magazine and jumped up pointing at it.

"What? What?" Pete shouted, as he jumped to his feet.

All Lily and Alyce could do was glance from the magazine to Pete with eyes wide, pointing at the picture. Pete looked over at it and asked, "Whoa. What's that?"

"I have no idea," answered Alyce. "We were just sitting here, listening to you play and the picture just started getting blurry and swirly."

Lily reached across and went to touch the photo. Alyce grabbed her arm and said, "Wait maybe we shouldn't touch it," as she cautiously closed the magazine and looked at them.

"Maybe we should go sit outside for a few minutes and get some fresh air," Lily suggested. "We're all getting a little sir crazy sitting up here," she continued, hoping Pete would agree.

"Exactly! Fresh air is what we need!" Alyce exclaimed. She was more concerned about the magazine at the moment. The talent show was the last thing on her mind. "We have to figure out what is going on with this thing," Alyce said as she stood up and waved it in front of them.

"Who cares about your dumb magazine, Alyce? We have more important things to do," Pete said grabbing his guitar, some sheet music and his newly sharpened pencil.

Alyce picked her camera up off the floor and put the strap around her neck. Lily picked up her backpack, and stuffed her sketch pad in it, and did a little dance in celebration of being allowed out to breathe some fresh air.

"One hour, you've got one hour to the figure this nonsense out," Pete said. "Then we are back to work," he continued. He narrowed his eyes and looked at them very seriously, "Do I have your word that we'll come back up here and work in an hour, and there will be no more goofing around?"

"Yes, of course, Pete," Alyce said absently. Her brain was going a mile a minute, and all she could think of was the swirling picture. "Let's go, Lily," Alyce said as she grabbed Lily's hand and stuffed the magazine into her backpack. The three of them headed for the door.

Pete reached for the doorknob and turned back one last time, saying to the girls, "One hour!" as he pulled his bedroom door open.

The door opened, and the three friends stood in silent amazement. Alyce rubbed her eyes, Lily held on to Alyce's hand and Pete stepped back and slammed the door shut. The room had gone pitch black. "Did you guys see that?" Pete asked. "What's going on?" he yelled into the darkness.

"I'm scared, Alyce," Lily said quietly and gripped Alyce's hand even tighter.

"Pete, open the door!" Alyce commanded.

"No way, Alyce! I'm not touching that doorknob again," Pete responded.

"I'll open it," Alyce said determinedly.

She let go of Lily's hand and pushed Pete aside. She took a breath and bravely pulled the door open again. Alyce stopped short in the doorway, with Lily close behind her. She let her breath out, in awe of the bright light.

PART II
Jules

CHAPTER 4
The Magazine

THEY SHIELDED THEIR EYES, TRYING TO BECOME ACCUSTOMED to the light, before they were able to observe their new surroundings. It appeared that they were standing in a wheat field that went on for miles. After a moment, Alyce took a few steps forward and surveyed the horizon. She then took out her phone and tried to check their location, but there was no service. "Hmm. That's going to be a problem," she said as she slipped her phone back into her pocket and turned to face Pete and Lily.

"Alyce, what just happened?" Pete asked, spinning around wildly, as he pointed in the direction of where his bedroom door used to be. It had completely vanished. "How do you explain this?" he asked, beginning to pace back and forth nervously. "Where are we?" he shouted out loud.

"I just want to go home. I'll even work on the talent show with no excuses. I just want to go home," Lily tearfully said dropping her bag onto the ground.

"It's not possible. It just can't be," Alyce mumbled to herself, while Pete and Lily just stared at her.

"What is it, Alyce? What happened?" Pete asked as he stopped and stood still for a moment.

"I know this is going to sound crazy, but I think we went through the picture in the magazine," Alyce answered assuredly, looking at the two of them.

Lily gasped, and Pete began pacing again through the waist high grass with a scowl on his face. The grass was so tall that Lily had to jump to see over it. "Can I please have the magazine out of your backpack, Lily?" Alyce requested.

"Sure, Alyce," Lily tearfully responded.

She picked up the bag to hand to Alyce, when she noticed that the backpack was a lot lighter than before. She opened it quickly and peeked inside. Her mood completely shifted when she saw her stuff was gone!

"What did you do with my stuff Pete?" Lily asked in an accusatory tone.

"Stuff? What stuff?" Pete answered. "I don't know what you're talking about."

"My stuff! Lily exclaimed.

"I may have accidentally taken a thing or two out when I was looking for the pencil," Pete said, looking away from Lily's stare.

"Well, it looks like you forgot to put those things back in," Lily said angrily narrowing her eyes at Pete.

"Enough, you two," Alyce said as she took the backpack from Lily and began searching through it.

She took the magazine out of the bag, and she removed her camera from around her neck, and carefully placed it inside Lily's bag. She didn't bring her case for it, because she didn't know they would be traveling.

Pete dropped down to the ground and began rambling on and on to himself about their situation. A moment later, Alyce joined him on the ground and frantically began flipping through the magazine. When she found the page she was looking for, she jumped up, holding the magazine open, comparing it to the landscape in front of her. "I knew I wasn't imagining things," Alyce said with certainty. "Look at the horizon. Now look at this," Alyce said, pointing to the picture in the magazine, showing them. "Coincidence?" she asked, raising her eyebrows.

"No way! Do you hear what you're saying, Alyce?" Pete said, jumping to his feet and looking around. "You think we're in a magazine?" he continued. "I think you watch too many science fiction shows, because I know I'm in some freaky dream, and I'm going to wake up any second," he said, pinching his arm, trying to wake himself up to no avail. "Come on, Pete. Snap out of it! Wake up!" he said, while pinching himself with his eyes closed. "You're going to open your eyes, and you'll be back in your room," he said. He opened his eyes, and he was still standing in the same field now, with Alyce standing there with her arms crossed.

"Well, Pete, that didn't work too well," Alyce said. "I didn't say we were in a magazine, I said I think we fell through a magazine. I suggest that we start walking."

"Wait... where's Lily?" Pete asked, looking around.

"She was just here a minute ago," Alyce replied, looking around.

Pete called Lily's name and got no response. "Come on, Lil, I'm not in the mood for this! We just fell through a magazine!" Pete exclaimed.

Up ahead he saw something moving in the field. A second later out popped Lily, with a handful of wildflowers, slowly walking back to them. Pete waved his arm over his head and yelled to Lily, "Hello little flower girl. Can you step on it?" he asked.

Lily wandered back over to Pete and Alyce. "Look at these beautiful flowers I found. I think I'll make a headpiece," she said, showing them to Pete.

"Oh, brother!" Pete said. "This one is telling me we went through a magazine," he said while pointing at Alyce, "and this one is wandering off picking flowers. Is anyone here understanding the seriousness of this situation?" Pete shouted, glancing from Lily to Alyce.

"If you let me explain, instead of huffing and mumbling, maybe you would understand what I'm talking about," Alyce said excitedly. She turned around, looked at the landscape and turned back to them, "Yes, I think when I opened the magazine, I accidentally opened some kind of portal," she said seriously. Pete continued to shake his head. Alyce continued, "This place is the exact picture of what I was looking at when things got all freaky."

"Where did you get that magazine, by the way, Alyce?" Pete questioned, as he narrowed his eyes and turned towards her.

"The Amatoli's! The Amatoli's!" shouted Lily, before Alyce could answer.

"Of course! The Amatoli's. The same family that disappeared without a trace under suspicious conditions. Today of all days, you decide to pick up their mail. Great, job Alyce!" Pete shouted as he slapped his forehead.

Lily stood there smiling and glanced down at her flowers, as Pete and Alyce continued to argue. Pete thought to himself, "One minute I was working on the talent show, the next I'm through some magazine portal, and wound up somewhere that isn't New Jersey." he thought to himself. "Where to now, genius?" he asked, getting right into Alyce's face.

"Yeah, Alyce," Lily said. "This is your fault."

"Hush, you two, and Pete step off," Alyce replied, as she pushed Pete back away from her.

"Fight! Fight!" Lily shouted taunting them.

Alyce and Pete looked at each other and then at Lily, and the three just started laughing. Alyce held up the magazine photo trying to match their surroundings, and said, "If we walk a little to the right, there appears to be a road of some kind."

"Ok, Alyce, now you're a tour director?" Pete questioned sarcastically.

"Yeah, Alyce," Lily repeated. "This is your fault."

Alyce just glared at both of them, stuffed the magazine into her back pocket. She handed Lily her bag, and said, "I'm heading to the road. You can follow me if you want, or you can stand there and argue."

Pete and Lily looked at each other and shrugged their shoulders. Pete swung his guitar around his back, and they followed Alyce through the field to the road ahead.

CHAPTER 5

Pardo'n

ONCE THEY HAD REACHED THE DIRT ROAD, ALYCE STOPPED and looked to the left, then to the right. "Which way now, genius?" Pete questioned.

Lily took a sniff of the air and said, "Let's go to the right. I smell something delicious that way." Pete and Alyce looked at her sternly. She shrugged her shoulders and said, "Because right can't be wrong," she continued.

"Hold on, hold on. Let me get my bearings for a minute," Alyce replied loudly. She looked from her right to the left, and said, "This way," pointing to her left.

"Are you sure this is the right way, Alyce? I sure am getting hungry," Lily complained.

"Enough! Enough! Alyce is following a magazine, and you are thinking about food, Lily," Pete shouted. "Don't I get a say in which way we go?" he demanded.

Alyce and Lily started to head left. Pete threw his hands up into the air in frustration and followed them silently.

They continued to disagree about which was the right way to go. Pete came to an abrupt halt and turned to Alyce and Lily. "I'm not taking another step until we figure out what is going on."

"Somehow this magazine transported us here. That's all I know," Alyce said. "I think we should just keep walking and see what is up ahead."

Alyce started walking and Pete and Lily followed, without saying a word. Pete heard Lily sniffling and tapped her on her shoulder. She turned to him with her lower lip quivering and asked with tears in her eyes, "How are we ever going to get home?" Pete grabbed her hand and squeezed it.

"It will be alright Lil," he assured her, and they continued to walk.

Alyce stopped suddenly and looked in the other direction. She looked at Pete and Lily nervously as they gathered around her. "What's the matter, genius? What? Are we lost?" Pete asked.

Before Alyce could respond, Lily pipped in saying, "It's impossible to be lost, when you don't even know where you are."

"Oh, brother, I can't deal with this. Just get me home, Alyce," Pete said.

They continued to walk following the road, when out of the tall grass a young boy popped out right in front of them. The boy jumped back, startled, when he saw them on the road. Alyce and Lily were caught off guard, causing them to trip over each other. They tumbled to the ground before Pete had a chance to catch them. The boy rushed over, hoping that the girls weren't hurt. "Whoa, where did you come from?" Pete asked surprised, while he reached down helping Lily to her feet.

The boy said, "Pardón," as he helped Alyce up. She dusted herself off and readjusted her eyeglasses on her head.

"Do you know where we are?" Pete nervously asked.

The boy looked at Pete strangely before answering and said, "You're in France."

"France!" the three friends echoed in astonishment and looked back and forth at one another. There had to be another explanation.

"Oui," the boy answered. "France".

"How is this possible?" Pete asked out loud.

Alyce turned towards him and answered through her grinding teeth, "I told you Pete, we went through this magazine," she said, waving it in the air.

Pete glared at Alyce, then turned towards the boy and said, "Hey, I'm Pete."

"I'm Lily. This is Alyce," she said pointing at her, "and I bet your name is 'Dreamy'!" she said, winking at him.

"Pardón? Je m'applle 'Jules', I do not know this 'Dreamy' you talk of. I don't understand your slang," Jules said with an accent.

Jules was dressed in overalls and a wide brimmed hat. He was carrying a bag over his shoulder that was filled with fruits and vegetables. He was about their age. He had short dark brown hair and light blue eyes. His skin was tanned from working outdoors.

"You can tell me about your current situation on the way back to my house. It's only another few minutes down the road," he said, leading the way. Pete, Lily and Alyce followed him.

After walking for a few moments, Jules asked Pete how they got there. Pete turned to Jules and said, "I'm going to tell you a story that you are not going to believe." Jules urged him to continue. "Alyce believes we fell through a magazine she found, and somehow we wound up here," Pete loudly said to Jules and asked him, "How do you say, 'crazy idea' in French?" Alyce stopped walking and halted the group by holding up her hand.

"Stop! It's my magazine," she said. "I'll tell the story." Taking a deep breath, she said, "It started when I found it on a very strange neighbor's driveway."

"I told her not to pick it up," Lily interjected, winking at Jules. "I warned her," she continued.

They all agreed to discuss their dilemma once they had gotten settled back at Jules' house. They continued walking in silence and saw cows and horses grazing in the pasture. Sheep were resting under a shady tree.

Alyce and Lily were looking around, enjoying the landscape. Lily wished they could stop for a while, so she could sketch the beautiful scenery, but this group seemed to be in a rush. They walked past lemon trees, grape vineyards and olive groves. "Pick whatever you can reach," Jules said, as they walked by the orchards.

Alyce started picking apples and pears that hung over the side of the road. Lily jumped up and tried to reach the trees but couldn't. "Guess you jumping for the trees is fruitless!" Pete said turning towards her barely getting the sentence out without falling over in laughter. Alyce cracked up along with Pete. Lily stuck her tongue out at them both, as Alyce handed her an apple. She wiped it off and took a bite.

"Boy, I was starving," said Lily dramatically. Pete and Alyce ignored her, as their new friend looked on with amusement.

They continued walking in silence for a few moments and saw a large barn up ahead. Alyce looked around and started turning slowly in a circle and said, "No way!" as she grabbed for the magazine in Lily's backpack.

"Alyce! What's with this going in and out of my bag every two minutes? Why don't you get your own?" she shouted.

Alyce began searching for the specific page in the magazine. When she found it, she tapped Pete on his shoulder and handed it to him. He looked at the photo and looked around and handed it back to Alyce without commenting. He wasn't about to show Jules that crazy magazine, at least not yet. Alyce folded the magazine in half and stuck it in her other back pocket.

CHAPTER 6
The Barnyard

SUDDENLY, ONE OF THE FARMHANDS RAN OUT OF THE BARN, frantically yelling to Jules in French. Jules began to run towards the barnyard, with Pete, Alyce and Lily following close behind. As he ran, he explained to them that three baby goats were missing. They had somehow gotten out of the pen. The friends immediately offered their help to find the goats. They left their belongings in the barnyard and ran after Jules into the nearby fields. They spread out in search of the babies.

Every time they thought they had one captured, it would slip away. Pete, Alyce and Jules were running in circles, trying to catch the goats with their hands, and each time they slipped away. After countless attempts, they gave up, and they all collapsed in a heap, laughing together.

Jules stood up and helped his friends to their feet. They all began walking back to the barn. "They'll return. When they're hungry, they'll come home. Let's go to my house, so I can talk to my mother and let her know there will be three more for dinner," Jules said.

"Speaking of three, has anybody seen Lily?" Pete asked.

"Once she smells the dinner, she'll find her way back," Alyce said laughing.

Moments later they saw Lily walking up the road towards the barn with the three baby goats trailing behind her. She guided them into the open pen, where they joined the others. Pete, Alyce and Jules looked at her with their mouths opened. "What? I got bored and started picking flowers to make a headpiece, when out of nowhere, some crazy baby goats attacked me and tried to steal my flowers. I chased them onto the road, and they started following me back to the barn. I tried to get away, but they followed me all the way here. I hope they are yours," Lily answered.

"Do you believe this?" Pete exclaimed "We are running around in this grass like fools and she has them following her home, like she's the Pied Piper." Alyce laughed and Jules smiled and shrugged his shoulders. Jules, Pete and Alyce stood there in amazement. Lily turned, looked at them, and said, "What?" She threw her hands up in the air. "What is the big deal? Why are you looking at me like that?"

"Lily, I don't know about you sometimes," Pete said, shaking his head.

Jules secured the gate to the pen, and they started up the path up to his house. The house was made from stone, and you could tell that it had been standing for generations. It had wide windows that swung open and a huge wooden front door. There was green ivy that grew all the way up to the chimney, and the house was surrounded by tall trees that had to be centuries old. Jules explained his family made wine that they sold at the farmers' market every day, with fresh food and milk.

He turned to them and said, "I'm going to tell my mother that you are foreign exchange students from America, and it's my weekend to host them. I will apologize to her and tell her I forgot, so go with this story. "

They followed him into the house, as Alyce lingered for a moment to snap a quick photo of the exterior of the house with her phone. She quickly joined them in the kitchen, where a woman was cooking. Pete took a sniff, and his stomach grumbled. "It smells so good in here," Alyce said.

"Yeah I'm getting hungry," Lily said out loud.

Pete motioned to Lily with his pointer finger to come stand next to him. Jules explained to his mother who they were. He hugged his mother, and she turned around with a French accent, she said, "Welcome to our home."

Alyce thanked her, and Pete and Lily gave her a smile. As Jules led them upstairs, Pete asked in a hushed whisper, "Are you sure this is okay?"

"Yes, everything is fine, and my mother is happy to have guests." Jules replied and showed them to the 'toilettes' where they could clean up.

Jules told them he was going down to the kitchen to help his mother finish with dinner. Once they were done, he said to come downstairs and he would show them where they would be eating.

CHAPTER 7
French Fun

THE THREE WASHED UP AND HEADED DOWN THE STAIRS. JULES was there waiting for them. He showed them where they could leave their belongings and led them into the dining room. They passed under an arched doorway into a large room. There was a fireplace at the far end. In the middle there was a long, beautiful, wood carved table, surrounded by six chairs with blue cushions. "My mom sits here," he said, as he pointed to the head of the table. "I sit there," he said, indicating the chair to the right, "so feel free to sit anywhere else." He then returned to the kitchen to help his mother.

"Don't even think about it, Alyce." Lily said, knocking her out of the way, as she ran next to the vacant seat next to Jules. She plopped herself down in the chair and smiled smugly at Alyce.

"What is the matter with this one?" Pete quietly asked Alyce, as they walked to their seats.

"She is just being Lily. I think she's crushing on Jules," Alyce whispered to him as she sat down.

Mrs. Sinclair and Jules emerged from the kitchen, carrying a bunch of platters which they placed on the table. One consisted of a mixed salad that was made fresh from the vegetables on their farm. The other platter had a delicious smelling roast and another plate of baked potatoes. Jules and his mother took their seats and began passing the platters around the table, family style, so everyone could help themselves.

Jules's mother explained over dinner about their farm and the history of the house. It had been in the family for generations. She told them about all the different crops they grew there and how they sold their produce and dairy in the local market. Jules's mom makes jams and jellies, soaps, and other handmade items, that she has Jules sell at the market as well.

She asked them a lot of questions about America, since she believed they were foreign exchange students. She wanted to know about California, because of the wine production there. It was such a beautiful night, Mrs. Sinclair suggested they have dessert out on the patio. Jules left the room for a second, and Alyce joined him. He returned with a harmonica and Pete's guitar. Alyce returned with her camera. Jules handed Pete his guitar and said, "Come on," and led them outside. He then explained that his harmonica belonged to his dad, who had passed away, and it was a gift from his mother.

They sat outside, enjoying their dessert, which was homemade eclairs, as they listened to French music playing on the radio. Pete began to strum along to the music playing. Jules joined in with his harmonica, tapping his foot along with the beat. Mrs. Sinclair and the girls chatted quietly, while the boys played. They had a fun night with good food, music and their new French friend.

Jules's mother looked at the time, and it was close to midnight. Before she could send them off to bed, Alyce asked for a group photo. Mrs. Sinclair happily took it. She then showed them out to the barn, with a stack of blankets, apologizing that she did not have room in the house. Pete said, "It's all cool, Mrs. Sinclair," taking the blankets from her and giving her a thumbs up. She smiled and suggested that Jules should take them into the city tomorrow to see the sights.

Jules picked up a lantern and walked them out to the barn. He opened the barn door and said, "Bienvenüe a la maison," which translates to 'Welcome home' in French. Pete, Alyce and Lily looked around at their new surroundings.

"So, where do we sleep?" Pete asked.

"In the loft," Jules replied.

Lily was yawning widely, and Alyce could barely keep her eyes open. She grabbed the pile of blankets from Pete, and with her camera around her neck, she headed up the ladder to make the beds. Lily looked around and asked, "One question, Jules. Where is the bathroom?" He misunderstood her question and responded, "You will have to wait until tomorrow."

Lily looked around, then looked at Jules and said under her breath, "Okay."

Jules looked around and bid them goodnight and said, "I'll see you in the morning, my friends. Remember, tomorrow we are going into the city by train, so we need to leave early."

They said goodnight to Jules, as he closed the barn door and left the lantern with them. Pete said to Lily, "Alright, get up there, kid," and she climbed up the ladder.

He placed his guitar behind his back and went to make sure the door was locked. Alyce finished making up the bed, and Lily jumped right into the middle and dove under the blanket, saying, "Aaaah." Lily got herself comfortable in the makeshift hay bed, and as soon as her head hit the hay, she was fast asleep. Alyce shook her head and jumped in next to her, leaving no room for Pete. A minute later, Alyce was softly snoring too.

Pete made sure the front door was secured and climbed up the ladder. "Hey, Alyce, Jules agrees with your theory that we teleported here while we were looking at the magazine together," Pete said. "Maybe we should show him the magazine tomorrow. What do you think?" he asked and got no response. He turned, looked at them both, and discovered they were sound asleep and hogging all the blankets. "These two are going to make me crazy," he mumbled under his breath, as he laid down in a stack of hay. "Wait until I get these two in the morning. How are they asleep so easily? It's not exactly normal to travel through a magazine, but they don't seem to be worried," he thought to himself.

Pete stayed awake most of the night, tossing and turning, worried about their current dilemma. He finally fell asleep right before dawn. He had only slept for an hour, when he was jolted awake by the loud crow of a rooster that was standing right next to his head. He jumped up, with hay sticking out of his hair, and shouted at the rooster, "Get lost!"

CHAPTER 8
A Day in The City

"RISE AND SHINE, SLEEPING BEAUTIES," PETE SAID IN A cranky tone. He clapped his hands loudly over the girls' heads, and they finally began to stir.

"What time is it?" Alyce asked, sitting up and rubbing her eyes.

"Huh," Lily mumbled incoherently, still half asleep.

"I don't know," said Pete "It's way early. That's all I know, and you two need to get up."

A few minutes later they heard Jules shouting from the barnyard, "Are you awake my friends?" Alyce and Lily were now more awake, folded up the blankets quickly, and carried them down the ladder, with Pete following behind them.

"Why do you look so tired?" Lily asked Pete, noticing the dark circles under his eyes.

"Why do I look so tired,' she asks?" he answered with a huff. Pete began to explain how she and Alyce hogged the whole sleeping area and all the blankets.

"Why didn't you just use the blanket in my backpack?" Lily asked holding her bag opened to show him.

"What blanket?" Pete asked, taking a quick glance.

"This one, right here," Lily was about to say, when she realized the blanket wasn't there.

"You must have left it behind in your room," Lily said angrily.

"It's too early for this," Alyce said as she placed the stack of blankets on a wooden counter in the barn.

Just then, Jules swung open the barn door and greeted them with a "Happy good morning." He explained that he had to quickly complete his chores, so they could leave for the train as soon as possible. He instructed Lily and Alyce on how to collect the eggs and put out fresh chicken feed. Pete and Jules put fresh hay into the stalls and fed the goats. Once they were done, they quickly washed their hands. They went back into the barn, grabbed their belongings, and jumped into the wagon, where Jules was waiting for them. He quickly introduced them to Andre, who was one of the farmhands. As soon as they were settled in the wagon, Jules passed them back a small picnic basket. Inside were fresh baked croissants with jam, cheese, grapes and warm sweet milk. The group quickly devoured the delicious breakfast, as they watched the beautiful scenery go by.

The wagon was also full of fresh fruits and vegetables that Andre would bring into town to sell at the local market. Jules brought them to his usual stand, and they helped Andre set up. After they were finished unloading the wagon, they took a stroll through the aisles of the market, since they still had an hour to spare.

The sights and sounds around them were wonderful. Some farmers sold fruit and vegetables, while some sold fresh eggs, milk and cheese. Others sold wine or homemade jams. Some were selling natural remedies, ointments, and soaps. A few women had stands that sold handmade knitted goods, like sweaters, scarfs and blankets. Others sold beautiful lace items and other vintage trinkets. There were several men gathered at their stands, selling seeds and small farming tools.

Alyce wandered up and down the rows, as she snapped pictures of all the colorful sights. "These are going to be great for the show," Alyce said excitedly. The smell of fresh bread and pastries lingered in the air, and Lily's stomach began to growl. "Really, Lily!" Alyce said. "We just finished breakfast!"

"I know. It just smells so good!" Lily said, taking a whiff of the air.

"Come on. Let's go find Pete and Jules," Alyce said, grabbing Lily's hand.

Pete and Jules were walking a short distance ahead. Jules stopped at one of the stands and spoke to the young girl behind the wooden counter. She took the picnic basket and began to fill it with mouthwatering goodies. Lily ran to join Jules and instructed him on what to get. Pete and Alyce just laughed, as Jules picked up the basket and guided them out of the market and towards the train station.

They walked through the station, and Jules went to the counter and retrieved their tickets. The group walked down the stairs and towards the platforms. They reached platform 23 in just a few minutes, and they sat down on one of the wooden benches. "This architecture of this building is amazing!" Alyce exclaimed, as she took picture after picture. "And the people are absolutely fascinating," she continued.

"Yeah, whatever, Alyce," Pete said as he yawned widely.

Within minutes they heard the rumble of the approaching train. The whistle blew, as the train pulled into the station. The doors opened, and they climbed aboard with Jules in the lead. They easily found four empty seats together, sat down and stored their belongings. Just as they got settled, Lily whined, "I can't ride backwards. I'll hurl for sure."

Alyce got up in a huff and changed seats with her. The train doors closed quickly, and they were slowly moving out of the station. "Here we go my friends," Jules said.

Lily and Alyce sat across from each other, looking out the window. Pete sat alongside Jules. He pointed out the sights of the different towns and villages to them, as the train passed through them. He asked if they were hungry, and Lily raised her hand and said, "I am. I am." Even Jules shook his head and laughed now at her constant hunger.

He took out their lunch, which consisted of fresh bread, pastries, cheese, grapes and pieces of dark chocolate. They ate, as they told him stories about America and talked about meeting him in New York one day.

They cleaned up from their lunch and rode the rest of the way in silence. Pete dozed off, and Alyce closed her eyes for a few minutes to think. She still could not understand how any of this was possible. How did they travel through a magazine? By now they had been gone for two days. That meant it was Sunday. By now their families had to be worried sick. What were they going to tell the police? She thought, "Well, Officer, they went into Pete's room and disappeared. We never saw them again." This had to be causing mayhem at home, Alyce thought nervously.

Lily was chatting away with Jules, filling him in on all the American celebrity gossip. She also told him about their school and the dance. She whispered to Jules, "This guy is making us miss the dance, all because of this talent show." Lily continued, as she nodded towards Pete and said, "He's a real downer, if you know what I mean, Jules."

"Yes, a misérables," he replied, and he and Lily just laughed and laughed.

The train began to slow down, and the conductor announced the upcoming stop. Jules smiled at them and said, "Let's go my friends. We have much to see." The train came to a full stop. They grabbed their stuff, and stood up, and waited for the doors to open.

"Lily, don't forget your backpack, please," Pete said sternly. They followed Jules off the train and onto the platform. Jules glanced around for the exit and motioned for the group to follow him.

He led them through a small tunnel that was absolutely spotless and up a flight of stairs that led out on to the street. They shielded their eyes when they walked out into the bright sunlight and looked around. Alyce immediately got her camera out and began to click away at all the unique structures and buildings they passed. They walked through the twisting and turning alleys that were really roads for the locals. They were amazed by the teeny tiny cars and how they sped through the little narrow streets. Many people used bicycles or small mopeds to get around easily. In the main part of the city, they still used electric cable cars that ran on wires strung across the city streets. Jules explained how the country was developing new cable cars that would still run on electricity, but more efficiently.

After seeing many of the sights, including a museum and several beautiful fountains, the group decided to start heading back to the station. Jules suggested they stop at his favorite dessert place on the way back to the train. Lily squealed with excitement, "French ice cream! I'm in!"

"Of course, you are, Lily" said Pete, Alyce and Jules in unison.

They ordered their ice cream and asked the waiter to take their photo with Alyce's camera. They sat at an outdoor table, so they could people watch for a while. Pete and Jules got into a conversation about a big upcoming soccer event. Lily sat back and began to sketch a small white cat that was sunning itself on the seat next to her, as she sipped on her vanilla milkshake. Once everyone had finished their ice cream, Jules looked at the clock in the town square and said, "Let's go. We can't miss the train."

They gathered their belongings and started quickly walking down the street towards the station. Pete looked and saw Alyce was right behind him, but Lily was still at the ice cream shop. "What are you doing Lily?" he shouted down the block. "We've got a train to catch in ten minutes!" he shouted even louder. Pete motioned to Jules to go ahead as he and Alyce waited for Lily.

Lily ran to catch up to them and said, "Sorry guys. I had to leave the rest of my milkshake for that poor little kitten. He was starving, and I felt so bad," Lily explained with a sad little face.

"That's great, Lily, but can you step on it?" Pete asked, as he rushed them down the street into the train station.

They looked on the schedule marquee and saw they were leaving from Platform 3. They followed the signs and quickly found Jules, who was waiting for them. He waved them over to the bench he was sitting on. "Ah you made it!" Jules exclaimed.

"Yes, thank goodness," Alyce said. "All are here and accounted for."

"Guitar?" Pete asked out loud. "Check," he replied. "Alyce, camera?"

"Check," she answered.

"Lily, backpack? Lily?" Pete asked, as he turned to look at her. "Now what?" Pete exclaimed.

They all looked at Lily, and she looked down embarrassed. "I think I left it at the ice cream shop, when I was feeding the cat," she barely whispered.

"You left it where?" Pete exploded.

"It was an accident, Pete!" Lily said with tears in her eyes.

"Lily!" Pete said through gritted teeth.

"Stop, Pete." Alyce said, "This is not going to help anything," as she motioned towards Lily.

Jules looked at the clock and interrupted the argument, "My friends, I don't mean to be rude, but I cannot miss this train. Someone must go back for the backpack quickly." Lily urged Pete and Alyce to go back to fetch the backpack so that she could have alone time with Jules. Pete and Alyce ran through the station, back towards the ice cream shop. Lily and Jules paced back and forth and hoped they would make it back from the dessert café in time.

Lily heard the rumble of the train, walked to the edge of the platform, and peaked over the side to see the approaching train. Jules grabbed her by the back of the shirt shouting, "Lily!" as he pulled her back from the edge.

"Thank you for saving my life, Dreamy!" Lily said, as Jules slapped his forehead and shook his head. They nervously waited until the final whistle blew.

"All Aboard." the conductor announced in French.

Jules looked at Lily and said, "I have to take this train. My mother is expecting me home to do the farm chores."

"We can't leave without them," Lily said loudly.

"Of course not," Jules yelled over the loud steaming of the engine. "Go to the ticket counter and change the three tickets to the next train. It is the last express of the day." He gave Lily a quick hug, hopped onto the train, and disappeared through the doors. She looked around nervously and walked towards the ticket counter.

PART III
Nallah

CHAPTER 9

Train Travels

Meanwhile, Pete and Alyce ran through the station out onto the street. They looked around and turned right. They ran two blocks and stopped at the corner, out of breath. "There it is, across the street," Pete said as he pointed to the opposite corner. They crossed the street and immediately went to the table where they had been sitting. They looked all around, under the table, on all the chairs. Nothing. The backpack was gone. Alyce looked at Pete and anxiously asked, "What do we do now?"

Pete shook his head and began to mumble under his breath, "It's always something. Nothing can ever go smoothly with these two." Their waiter came rushing towards them with the backpack in his hand.

"Merci," Pete and Alyce said together and took off running with it down the block.

Less than five minutes later, they were back at the station and headed towards the platform. Lily was sitting on the bench, looking around anxiously. "There she is!" shouted Alyce. Lily turned around and breathed a sigh of relief when she saw Pete and Alyce running towards her with her backpack.

"Hurry up you two," she shouted, as she jumped off the bench, "The train is about to leave! I've been waiting here for hours! What took you so long?" Lily complained.

"Where did Jules go?" Pete questioned Lily.

"He had to get back to the farm," she answered.

"Get on the train, Lily," Pete growled at her, as he handed her the backpack. They all climbed aboard, just as the doors slid closed behind them.

They found three seats together and sat down. Pete looked out the window, as the train slowly pulled out of the station. It was clear he was not in the mood for any conversation. Lily quietly explained to Alyce, who was putting her camera away, that Jules will have someone meet them at the station. The train blew its whistle, and they slowly pulled out of the station.

Fifteen minutes later, the train slowed down, and Pete tried to look out the window. It was impossible to hear the conductor over the loud screech of the brakes, but it seemed as if they were approaching a station. Pete looked at Alyce and said, "Isn't this the express train? I don't remember having any stops on the way here." Alyce looked at Pete and shrugged her shoulders. He then looked at Lily, who was sitting in her seat, humming a tune and flipping through her sketches. "I'm going to go find out what's going on. Lily, give me the tickets," Pete mumbled, as he got up and walked to the next train car.

Several minutes later Pete returned, with steam coming out of his ears. Alyce turned to look at him and said, "Pete, are you alright? What is it?"

"Lily exchanged our Express tickets for local tickets, which means this train ride is going to be about two hours longer, due to all the stops," he yelled at Lily.

"It was an accident, Pete. I know I'm smart, but I didn't learn French overnight. Jeez," and she rolled her eyes at him.

Alyce saw that Pete was furious. He was exhausted and worried about the show, so she tried to defuse the situation. "Okay, guys, it's not so bad. At least we're on the right train. We'll be late getting back, but Jules won't leave us stranded. Let's just try to relax. There's nothing else we can do except sit back and enjoy the ride," Alyce assured them.

Pete just stared out the window, muttering under his breath. He took out his guitar and started to tune it up a little. Lily took out her sketchpad and began to go over some of her drawings, while Alyce sorted through her pictures on her phone.

"Can you please grab me the magazine out of the backpack, Lily?" Alyce asked. Lily handed her the magazine, and Alyce began to flip through it.

"What are you doing with that thing? We're in enough trouble as it is. Put that magazine away," Pete demanded.

"Don't you want to see where we're going next, Pete?" Alyce taunted. She tossed the magazine, and it landed on the seat next to him. He looked down and saw the picture was of zebras and elephants, grazing on an African plain. He pushed the magazine away from him, and Alyce picked it up and put it away back into the backpack.

"What's the matter, Pete, are you scared of a little magazine?" Lily asked, egging him on.

They could barely hear the conductor's announcement over their continual arguing, and Lily insisted this was the right stop. They checked their seats to make sure they didn't leave anything behind, as they waited for the train to come to a complete halt. A second later, the doors opened, and a wave of heat enveloped them. They stepped out on to the platform, except it wasn't a platform, and they weren't in a train station either. The three friends looked at each other, and Pete said, "Hey Alyce, I don't think we are in France anymore." They all turned back, and the train they just exited was gone.

CHAPTER 10
Observing the Safari

THEY LOOKED AROUND, PUZZLED, TRYING TO FIGURE OUT WHAT had just happened. They were standing on a flat plain that was covered in dry brush. "Now this is beyond weird," Pete said taking another glance around and wiping the sweat off his face.

"You think?" Alyce said, looking around. "You were the last person looking at the magazine, Pete. What page were you looking at? What did you see?" she asked.

"I don't know. It was some picture with giraffes or something," Pete said.

"You mean like this?" she asked as she pointed at the giraffes, eating from a tall tree in the distance.

"Whoa!" Pete said, as he stood in disbelief.

"Here you go, Alyce," Lily said handing her the magazine out from her backpack, before Alyce could ask for it this time.

Alyce took the magazine without responding and began flipping through it.

"Here we go again," Pete said, throwing his hands up in the air as he began pacing back and forth.

"Do you have any other explanation for what is happening? If you do, Pete, please help us out here," Alyce said.

Alyce finally found the page she was looking for and showed it to Pete. "Is this what you were looking at?" she asked.

"Correction, Alyce. I wasn't looking at your magazine. You kind of forced it on me. Don't blame me for this. This is all your fault," he said, wiping off his brow again.

"Listen Pete..." Alyce said, as she was interrupted in mid-sentence by a jeep that came zooming out of the brush. Pete jumped back, as the jeep zipped passed them, and he quickly pushed Lily out of way, knocking her to the ground. Alyce looked at the two of them and shook her head. As the jeep came to a stop a few yards ahead of them, Alyce said, "I'm going to find out where we are."

"Wait, Alyce." Pete said cautiously. "We don't know who that is," he said.

"What are we going to wait for, Pete?" Alyce asked. "We need to find out where we are," she said.

"Send Pete over," Lily said in retaliation of Pete knocking her down.

"Somebody has to find out what is going on," Alyce said, as she ran ahead to the waiting jeep, leaving Pete and Lily behind.

"You want to give me a hand, Pete?" Lily asked, still laying on the ground, while Pete reached down and helped her to her feet.

"Sorry Lil," he said as he handed her the backpack.

They nervously waited, while Alyce walked up to the jeep.

Alyce approached the young girl behind the wheel, who she guessed was close to their age. She was dressed in safari attire, with her wild red hair poking out of the side of her safari hat. Alyce walked up to her and introduced herself, as Pete and Lily hung back and nervously watched from a distance. They could tell that they were in deep conversation and waited patiently for Alyce to wave them over. Alyce jumped into the jeep, and they made a U turn and drove back, where Lily and Pete were waiting. Alyce introduced everyone to Nallah and explained that they were in Africa.

"Africa!" Pete and Lily shouted in unison while Alyce nodded at them.

"Come on, get in!" Nallah said, as Pete and Lily climbed into the back seat of the jeep.

"Looks like you have been on a pretty wild trip." Nallah said, glancing back at them.

"That's only the half of it," Pete muttered under his breath.

Pete noticed the bumper sticker that read, "I love New York" with a heart replacing the word love. He said, "I know we traveled through a magazine, but what are you doing here? You're a long way from home, considering that we are in Africa." Nallah explained that her mother was an Elephant Conservationist, and her father was involved in well building projects, so they traveled around a lot.

They drove along the plain for a few minutes and pulled into a clearing. In the distance, they saw small raised huts scattered around a gigantic plain. She pulled into a small dirt parking lot and parked next to another jeep. "Oh, good, my mom is still here," Nallah said happily. "Let's go," she continued, as they all exited the jeep.

Nallah led the way down a narrow path, and the group followed. "Whew, it's hot!" Lily complained after they were walking for a few minutes. "I need some water."

"You're in Africa, Lily, not Antarctica," Pete replied sarcastically.

Lily shot him an angry look and stuck her tongue out at him. Nallah walked swiftly through the tall grass, and Lily shouted ahead to her, "How much longer, Nallah? I'm dying over here!"

"It's just another minute further," Nallah replied laughing.

Alyce lagged behind. She looked around and stopped every few seconds to take pictures of the new scenery with her phone. "This is amazing!" she thought to herself. She saw that the group was now out of sight, so she quickly put away her phone and ran ahead to join her friends.

"This place is incredible," Alyce said, as she looked around in awe and continued. "I can't believe you live here, Nallah."

"Wait till you see the elephants!" she answered excitedly.

They reached the raised hut, and Nallah began to climb expertly up the wooden ladder. "Come on, you guys!" she said. "Move it, move it." Lily went first and cautiously began to climb. She looked up, and Nallah said, "Don't worry, Lily. I'll help you." Lily reached the top, and Nallah pulled her up onto the platform. Nallah yelled down, "You're next, Alyce." Alyce looked at Pete and quickly climbed the ladder up into the hut. "Let's go, Petey Boy," Nallah said.

"On my way..." he was about to answer, but was interrupted by Lily.

"Yeah, come on, Pete. You're holding us up," Lily said peeking down through the hatch in floor of the hut.

"I'm coming," Pete yelled up as he grabbed the railing.

"Can you move any faster, Pete?" Alyce asked, as she yelled down to him, while he was about to grab the railing and start climbing up.

As Pete reached the top, he said, "I would have been up here sooner if the three of you would have stopped interrupting me. Geez, Now I have three girls bossing me around," Pete grumbled under his breath, while Alyce and Lily looked at him with their mouths hanging open, slightly embarrassed.

"Pete," Lily said as she kicked him in the ankle.

"Ouch!" Pete screamed.

"Around here, Pete, the girls are the bosses." Nallah smiled and winked at him in a teasing manner. Nallah was barely able to keep a straight face. Pete looked at the three of them, and they all burst out into loud laughter with Pete still rubbing his ankle.

"Nallah, is that you?" asked a woman's voice from inside the small hut.

"Yeah, Mom, I'll be right there," Nallah responded.

Nallah gathered the friends together on the opposite end of the platform and quietly said, "I'm going to tell my parents that you guys are thinking about doing a junior volunteer project here this summer, and you're here checking it out. That way she can't ask too many questions. Come on, I'll introduce you to her," Nallah said, as she led the way into the hut.

"Hey, Mom!" Nallah said.

"What have you been up to all day?" Nallah's mother asked, without looking up from the work on her desk. She turned to smile at Nallah and suddenly stopped and said, "Um, Nallah, is there something you're not telling me?" as she motioned towards the three friends. She had the same wild red hair poking through her safari hat and was dressed in the same exact outfit as Nallah.

"Mom, let me introduce you to Pete, Alyce and Lily. This is my mom, Dr. Sue, but you can just call her Sue," Nallah said and smiled at her mom. The three friends smiled at her mother.

"I'd offer you a proper shake, but as you can see, I'm up to my elbows in pink paint," Dr. Sue said, as she held up her paint covered hands.

"Is there anything to drink in this place?" Lily asked. Alyce and Pete both shot her a look, and she shrugged her shoulders. "What can I say? I'm thirsty."

Dr. Sue led them around to the other side of the observation deck and handed each of them a bottle of water. They took turns looking through the binoculars, as she pointed way out on the left side of the plain.

"You've painted their tusks pink!" shouted Lily. "Are they all girls?" she asked.

Dr. Sue laughed at Lily's question and answered, "No, that is the only color we have." Smiling at Lily, she then went on to explain that first they tag the elephants, and once that is done, they log them in a book, and usually give them a name.

"That is so cute. I wish I could pick an elephant's name," Lily said as she began to pout.

"Knock it off, Lily," Pete growled under his breath.

Dr. Sue continued, "Once they are tagged, we will have them tranquilized for a short time. We wait until they are sleeping, and then we paint their tusks with nontoxic paint, making the ivory useless to poachers. That is our goal here, to observe and preserve these beautiful animals. Unfortunately, it is already past grazing time. Maybe you can catch them tomorrow."

Nallah spoke to her mother privately for a minute, as Pete, Alyce and Lily looked at the beautiful sights.

"Why don't you take them down to see the newest addition while you're here?" Dr. Sue said as they emerged from the hut.

"Yes, for sure," Nallah said, hugging her mom.

The three friends thanked Dr. Sue and made their way down the ladder. "See you back at camp," Nallah yelled up to her mom.

"What's the newest addition?" Lily asked curiously.

"You'll see," answered Nallah, as she led them towards a few enclosed stalls.

"Not another goat, I hope. We had enough of the goats with Jules," Lily loudly said.

"Would you hush up?" asked Alyce as she grabbed Lily's hand.

"Here we are," said Nallah in a softer voice. "He's still getting used to people, so don't get too close," she warned, as they all looked at each other a little nervously.

They rounded the corner, and there in the stall was a baby elephant with its mother.

"How cute!" Lily said as she rushed towards the stall. "Can I pet him?"

"LILY!" Nallah shouted sternly. "I told you not to get too close. He's not used to a lot of people yet!"

"But he's so adorable," Lily exclaimed, as she reached into the stall to try to pet him.

"Don't you ever listen?" Alyce hissed and pulled her hand back.

At that point, it seemed as if the baby elephant had had enough. He took a big drink of water, used his trunk as a hose, and aimed it right at Lily.

"See, maybe he wants to say 'hello.' He's looking right at me," Lily said excitedly, as she moved a step closer to the stall. The baby elephant lifted his trunk and began spraying Lily. She backed up from the stall, but it was too late. She was already soaking wet from head to toe. Alyce, Pete and Nallah were laughing so hard that they couldn't breathe. They tried to compose themselves, when they looked at Lily standing there dripping wet with the biggest pout on her face.

"Are you still thirsty now, Lil?" Pete asked, and the three of them broke into uncontrollable laughter once again.

While they were still laughing, Lily started looking through her backpack for the extra tee shirt she carried. She searched to no avail, and the tee shirt was nowhere to be found. She looked up and glared at Pete. "What?" he asked.

"You dummy, when you pulled the blanket out, you must've pulled my tee shirt out too. Now I have nothing to change into," Lily answered.

"I'm sure I have something you can wear back at my hut. Come on. Let's go, guys," Nallah said.

The four of them walked quickly back to the jeep and hopped in. Five minutes later, they pulled into the camp and parked. "Oh, good, my dad's back," Nallah said as she turned off the engine.

CHAPTER 11

Base Camp

"WELL, WE'RE HERE," NALLAH SAID.

"What is this place?" Alyce asked.

"This is my hut, and my parent's hut is the one right next door," Nallah answered.

"Why are the huts raised? Why don't you just sleep in a tent?" Pete asked.

"You can sleep on the ground if you want Pete, that's if

you don't mind sharing a sleeping bag with a python or a scorpion," Nallah answered.

Alyce and Lily laughed. "Seriously though, at night you do have watch out for some interesting creatures,"

Nallah warned. She led Lily up the ladder to get her some dry clothes and left Pete and Alyce to look around below.

"This place is so interesting, isn't it, Pete?" Alyce asked as she spun around.

"Yeah it is pretty cool," he responded as he sat down on a nearby rock and swung his guitar around and started to strum.

"Any inspiration yet?" Alyce asked.

"Not quite," answered Pete, "but I am working on it." Alyce replied with a smile as she leaned against the jeep and looked through some of her pictures from that afternoon.

Seconds later, Lily came bounding down the ladder with Nallah right behind her. Pete and Alyce took one look at Lily and burst out laughing. She was dressed in a new tee shirt that came down to her knees. She had a belt wrapped around her to keep the shirt from dragging on the ground. Lily huffed at them, "I can't help it if I'm short."

"Just kidding Lil," Pete said as he ruffled her hair.

"Follow me," Nallah said as she led the way towards the main camp.

"Remember, you guys are checking out the camp for a junior volunteer summer project," Nallah reminded them.

They gave her a thumbs up, as they followed her toward the large tent set up in the center of the camp. She waved to several of the workers, as they stared curiously at the newcomers. Pete, Alyce and Lily looked around, as they approached the large tent. Nallah stopped to speak to a young boy in the local language, and the two of them laughed. He held the flap open, and she motioned for her friends enter.

They walked into the tent, with Nallah behind them. There were several people working at a few small folding tables scattered throughout the tent. A few men were gathered around a long table discussing how much further they had to dig. One of the men looked up and smiled as he saw Nallah. She waved at him, and he excused himself from the group and walked towards them. He scooped Nallah up in a big hug. She said, "Hi Dad! I missed you!"

"I missed you, too, Pumpkin," he said, and he squeezed her tighter. He pulled her away, looked at her and asked, "Are you behaving yourself?"

"Of course, Dad!" Nallah answered nodding her head. "I'd like you to meet my friends: Pete, Alyce and Lily. This is my dad, Dr. Stephen."

"Nice to meet you, kids, and please call me 'Stephen," he said smiling at them.

Nallah quickly explained why the friends were there, and her dad invited them to stay for the barbeque. "Hope it tastes as good as it smells!" Lily exclaimed and took a whiff of the air. The three friends and even Dr. Stephen laughed at Lily's remark.

Nallah led them to the buffet table and told them to grab a plate, help themselves, and meet her at one of the tables. Dr. Sue arrived shortly, and she and Dr. Stephen joined them. While they enjoyed the delicious food, Dr.

Stephen explained that he travels to villages and helps build wells to bring fresh drinking water to the locals. Her parents told them about how they met in school in New York because her mom lived there, and her dad was on a scholarship from Africa at the same time. Dr. Sue told story after story of their different projects that they did over the years. Alyce and Lily were absolutely mesmerized by the tales of their adventures all around the world.

Dr. Stephen led them outside to the campfire with Dr. Sue following behind carrying a bowl of fruit. She and Dr. Stephen were about to say good night, when Alyce jumped up and took her camera out of Lily's bag and asked them to take a picture of the four of them together in front of the campfire. Nallah's mom happily took the picture for them. She reminded them not stay up too late, they were going to the well tomorrow and it was a several mile walk. "Okay" the four friends answered together.

Once Nallah's parents walked towards their hut, the friends moved in closer around the campfire and Pete began to softly strum his guitar. "Okay you guys, now please tell me exactly how you got here. I know you said something about a magic magazine that brought you to France, then on a train, and now you're here in Africa?" Nallah asked curiously. Pete, Alyce and Lily all shook their heads up and down.

"Exactly!" Pete said continuing, "It's absolutely ridic-ulous. That's what I keep telling them. If there is a logical explanation of this, we haven't figured it out yet," Pete said.

"Okay, okay why you don't you start from the beginning," Nallah said.

They sat around the campfire filling her in on their journey so far. She was intrigued and asked to see the magazine. "No way! Don't you dare take that thing out again Alyce," Pete warned.

"Okay, let's not fight about it. Let's pick up the discussion tomorrow. You guys must be exhausted," Nallah said, as she noticed Alyce and Lily beginning to yawn.

"Yeah, I'm kind of beat," Alyce said, as she stood up.

She pulled Lily to her feet, and Nallah said, "Yeah, I think we better head off to bed, before this one starts sleep walking," motioning to Lily.

"Are you coming, Pete?" Alyce asked, as she picked up her camera and Lily's backpack.

"I'll be there, in a few," Pete answered as he stoked the fire. He needed a couple of minutes to himself to try to collect his thoughts.

As the girls headed off to bed, Pete sat back and looked up at the stars and softly strummed his guitar. The sky was beautiful. It reminded him of the time he visited his cousins in Colorado where they watched a meteor shower. He suddenly thought of the picture he had in his room. The one of the whole family up on top of the mountain, and he was instantly reminded that they were nowhere near home. His aunt must be frantic he thought.

"What about poor Oz? No one would even think about Ozzie," Pete thought nervously.

He was quickly brought back to reality, when he caught a young boy, walking through the camp out of the corner of his eye. The boy waved at Pete, and started walking towards him, Pete waved back. As he got closer, Pete could see that he was about six or seven years old, and he was carrying a small pail and two sticks. He sat down next to Pete and motioned for him to play. Pete began to strum the song he was working on for the talent show. The boy flipped the pail over and used the two sticks to begin drumming along with Pete. The beat of the drum put a whole new sound to Pete's song. He stopped playing for a second and scribbled some notes down on a piece of sheet music he kept in his pocket. The boy smiled, and Pete began to play and once again the boy joined in. They played for several minutes and finally Pete turned to the boy and said, "Okay, little man, I think you better get home now." The boy smiled at Pete, picked up his pail, and gave Pete a thumbs up. Pete slapped his leg, trying not to laugh, and gave the boy a thumbs up as well. The boy turned and headed home.

The campfire was just about out, as Pete kicked some dirt on the embers. He grabbed his guitar and the lantern that Nallah had left for him. The sounds of the young boy's drumming echoing in his head as he walked the short distance to the hut. As he approached, he noticed that Nallah had her jeep parked directly underneath the hut. Pete was too tired to even think about it, so he just shrugged his shoulders and made his way up the ladder.

CHAPTER 12

The Poachers

HE LOOKED UP AND SAW THAT THE HATCH WAS CLOSED, SO HE turned off the lantern and left it at the bottom of the ladder. He climbed up quickly and pushed the hatch open. Pete pulled himself up onto the platform and let his eyes adjust to the dark. He noticed that Nallah had left him some kind of blanket, a spray bottle of mosquito repellent and a note that said, "Sorry, Petey, the girls have the hut, but there's a comfy hammock on the other side of the deck."

Pete picked up the blanket and the bug spray. He stumbled through the dark to the other side of the platform, mumbling to himself as usual about the dilemmas that Lily and Alyce get him into. Pete easily found the hammock that was strung between two tall posts of the hut. He started to unfold the blanket and realized it wasn't a blanket at all. It was a mosquito net. "You've got to be kidding me!" Pete said out loud. "That's it, I've had it. They are on my last nerve," Pete continued to mumble as he tried to figure out how he was going to set up his "bed".

"First things first," Pete said to himself, as he slapped at the mosquito on the back of his neck. "Yuck," he thought as he wiped the huge mosquito guts on the railing of the platform. "These mosquitos are so big they need a license plate," he grumbled under his breath. He immediately sprayed himself from head to toe with the bug repellent and straddled the hammock. He sat down, with one foot on either side to balance himself. He reached down and pulled the netting over himself, trying to cover his entire body, but the netting was too short, and his legs and feet were fair game to the mosquitos. He sat up and tried to pull the netting down over his ankles, but it was stuck. He tugged a little harder and felt it starting to come loose as the hammock began to sway. He gave it one last tug, this time the hammock really began to swing back and forth. Pete was struggling to get a foot on the floor to balance himself. The netting came loose in his hand, and the entire hammock flipped over, and Pete went flopping on the floor with the net landing on top of him in a heap.

Pete laid on the floor for a minute, ready to blow his top. He tried to calm himself down because he didn't want to wake up the whole camp. He slapped at another mosquito and jumped up and grabbed the net. He was so tired and angry, all he cared about was getting some sleep right now. This time he wrapped himself in the net first and then maneuvered himself carefully back onto the hammock, being sure to keep his balance. He laid back and finally after some careful shifts and wiggles, he was finally comfortable. Pete could hear the mosquitos buzzing and bouncing off the net. "Out of luck suckers," he whispered as he drifted off to sleep.

He was abruptly woken up by a siren blaring about three feet from his head. He jumped up so quickly that he lost his balance and the whole hammock flipped again. This time Pete was entirely entangled, upside down like a spider's prey trapped in a web. He watched the girl's feet quickly scurry past him as he tried to free himself. By that time Nallah was already yelling, "Get up, get up! There're poachers nearby! Quick follow me." Nallah ran ahead and slid down the pole and into the jeep that was parked below.

As they heard the jeep roar to life, "Come on Lily, hurry up," Alyce said, grabbing onto the pole and sliding down. Just as Lily was about to slide down, she heard Pete saying, "Help me, I'm trapped!" Lily just looked at him and huffed.

"Now is not the time to imitate a spider Pete!" Lily said slightly annoyed.

"Just get me out of this thing!" Pete hollered as Nallah honked the horn from below.

"Pete has a slight problem up here, he's kind of stuck," Lily said as she looked down.

"Come on, we have no time to waste!" Nallah exclaimed as she revved the engine.

Lily disappeared to try to help free Pete from the hammock. She pulled the ropes loose untying him. "Let's go Pete! "Lily hollered as she slid down the pole. Alyce looked at Lily inquisitively as she saw Pete slide down, getting stuck every few inches due to the netting he was still entangled in. He finally flopped into the jeep with a thud. Nallah sped off with him still untangling himself from the remaining net.

Nallah said a bit annoyed, "I hope we didn't miss them! These guys are good, and it is the third time they've come back this week." She drove for a bit and then turned off her headlights and continued to drive slowly up a dirt road. She explained they were near the rear exit of the elephant's conservation site. Nallah asked, "Everybody ready?" Alyce and Lily shook their heads yes and Pete just sat there looking confused.

"Ready for what?" Pete asked.

"For the poaches you dummy. What did you think we were here for a night drive?" asked Lily sarcastically.

"Quiet!" Nallah snapped at the two of them.

A moment later she shouted, "Hit the lights Alyce!" A giant bright white spot light came on and lit the entire area. Alyce moved the light back and forth like Nallah instructed. Nallah jumped from the jeep to check the perimeter. She returned and instructed Lily to set off the flare indicating that poachers were in the area of the surrounding villages.

Nallah did one last loop around the perimeter and then returned them to camp in silence. Lily noticed that Pete was scratching like crazy. "Why didn't you use the bug spray? I used it and I don't have a single bite," Lily said, smirking.

"Yeah," Alyce said, "You do have an awful lot of bites...didn't you use the mosquito net?" Pete just shook his shoulders and didn't respond.

When they got back to the camp, the girls saw how tired Pete was, so they left a bed open for him inside. Nallah jumped in the hammock and Alyce and Lily shared the other bed inside the enclosed hut.

After getting a few hours' sleep, the group woke up somewhat refreshed considering the night they had. All Pete could think about was the long way to walk to the well and how tired he was. Nallah quickly dressed and told the group to hurry up and she would meet them at the main camp for breakfast.

The three friends quickly got ready, left the hut and met Nallah at the same table they had eaten at last night. After a quick breakfast, they were on their way to the well.

On their walk, Nallah explained the details of the well project and the work they were doing there. After a half hour of walking, Lily asked for a water break. "No, you don't get water until you get to the well." Nallah explained. "This way you can learn and be appreciative of how easily you have clean water and others don't."

"How much further?" Pete asked, wiping his brow mumbling.

"Another twenty minutes," Nallah answered.

They walked the rest of the way in silence. They spent a few hours with Nallah's father and the workers. He explained all about the wells, how they worked and how many villages would be benefiting from having access to clean water with this well.

Dr. Stephen was heading back to the home camp and offered to give the kids a lift. The ride back was quick and before they knew it, they were back at Nallah's hut. Lily, Pete and Alyce hopped out of the jeep. "Nallah, aren't you coming with us?" Alyce asked.

"Actually, I have to go back and help my dad with something, so I'll see you at dinner in fifteen minutes, don't forget to bring your stuff," she said as the jeep sped away.

"You don't have to remind me not to forget my guitar," Pete said as he led Alyce and Lily up the ladder.

When they reached the top, they went to gather their things to get ready for dinner. Alyce was thumbing through the magazine patiently waiting for Pete and Lily. Pete walked out of the hut and saw what Alyce was doing and said, "Really Alyce, we know this magazine is not normal, so leave it alone already". He pleaded.

Alyce was about to respond when she was interrupted by Lily's screaming.

"Help! Spider!" Lily yelled.

"Don't look at me!" Pete said, looking at Alyce. "I hate spiders."

Alyce dropped the magazine, and it fell to the floor with the page opened to a seaside village. Pete glanced down at the picture, "Why don't you use this to kill the spider," he said kicking the magazine closed.

"I am not going to kill it Pete," she said.

Alyce ran into the hut and Lily was standing on the cot yelling and pointing, "Spider! Spider!"

"Where? Where Lily?" Alyce asked.

"It's right there," Lily said, pointing at a teeny tiny spider the size of a grain of rice. Alyce looked at where Lily was pointing.

"You've got to be kidding me, Lily," Alyce said, as she grabbed her hand.

Lily picked up her backpack, and Alyce led her out the door to where Pete was waiting. "Does everyone have everything?" Alyce asked, picking up the magazine and handing it to Lily to put away.

"Are we ready now?" Pete asked getting annoyed with the delay.

Both girls nodded, as Pete reached down and gave the hatch a yank. Once the hatch was opened, Pete looked down into the darkness below. "I don't remember this looking like this last night," he said. "I'm not going first," he continued.

"Move out of the way, I'll go first, don't be a baby," Alyce said, gently pushing him away from the opened hatch.

She starting to climb down the ladder with Lily right behind her. Pete took one last look around nervously, threw his guitar on his back, and hoped that breakfast was at the bottom of this ladder and nothing else. He started to climb down the wooden steps and pulled the hatch closed above him.

PART IV
Song

CHAPTER 13

Down the Hatch

THEY CONTINUED TO DESCEND INTO THE DARKNESS BELOW. "Be careful guys. These rungs are getting slippery," Alyce warned holding on tightly.

"What do you mean getting slippery?" Pete asked out loud more to himself. "This is Africa it's hot and dry here," he said.

Suddenly, an overwhelming scent of the salty ocean filled their nostrils. "Oh no!" Pete exclaimed, recalling the opened page of Alyce's magazine, as he smelled the ocean air as well. He wiped the dampness from his hands onto his pants and readjusted his guitar on his back. He then continued down holding tightly with his other hand.

Alyce had reached the last rung and jumped off with a thud onto a wooden platform. "Just a few more steps down," Alyce instructed. Lily grew excited to see where they were and began to climb down faster.

"Slow down Lily before you slip," Pete said with concern.

"I've got her," Alyce said as she helped Lily off the last step.

Pete continued cautiously and reached where they were standing. Alyce looked around and assumed they were on a dock, considering they were surrounded by water and bobbing up and down. There were fishing boats of all sizes and colors anchored in the harbor, which explained why they smelled the ocean's air. They could hear the hustle and bustle a few feet above them. From their immediate surroundings, they had no idea where they were. Alyce pulled out the magazine and began flipping through it looking for the page that had been opened before leaving Nallah. "Where are we?" Pete questioned. "You're the tour director on this trip," he sarcastically answered in a tired and worn out voice.

"Don't you think I'm trying to figure that out Pete?" Alyce responded.

"I don't care where we are the food smells good," Lily said, as she tried to jump and get view of the activities above.

Pete nudged Alyce and motioned towards the young girl that was tying a small fishing boat to the dock. Alyce looked up and the girl started walking towards them.

CHAPTER 14
The Repair

THE THREE OF THEM LOOKED AT EACH OTHER AS SHE BEGAN TO slowly approach them. She appeared to be their age and had long, straight, jet-black hair. She was dressed in jeans and a sweatshirt and was carrying a small bucket in her hand. Pete, Alyce and Lily smiled and waved at her. She returned the smile and waved back. As she got closer, she observed Pete's guitar and asked, "Are you here for the wedding?"

"Not exactly," Pete answered.

"So, what brings you here?" Song asked.

Alyce did the introduction and explained briefly to Song what had been happening to them and the places they'd been. Song was very intrigued and looked at them and said, "I'd like to hear more but I have to get my fish to market before it closes. So, follow me." She proceeded to lead them up the ladder and helped them onto the cobblestone street above. Pete reached the top and noticed that his shoelace had come undone. He bent down to tie it and all of a sudden there was a loud pop!

"What was that?" Lily asked.

"Don't tell me. Don't tell me," Pete said holding his head with his eyes closed.

"Uh huh." Lily said nodding her head, looking at his guitar.

"Which one is it?" Pete asked anxiously.

"Hello, I don't play guitar," she said sarcastically. "It's the second string," she continued.

"Yup. That's the B." Pete said sadly.

Pete slowly stood up and took his guitar strap off his neck. He checked his string and saw that indeed one string had broken and hung his head in despair. "By any chance, is there a music shop anywhere in town," Pete asked with hope in his eyes.

"No, I'm sorry," Song said, "but I do know someone who may be able to fix it. First, I must drop off my fish, then, I will take you to her," Song said.

As they walked, she explained that there was a big wedding in town that evening, and everyone was invited. She went on to tell them that her grandmother was the local seamstress and had a small shop in town. Her grandmother would be busy preparing for tonight's wedding because she was doing the finishing touches on the bride's gown. She then stopped in front of a small stand and instructed them to wait as she hurried inside to drop off the bucket of fish.

Lily and Alyce walked a little further up the street to investigate while they waited. Pete sat on the curb, sadly holding his guitar in his arms. After a moment, Song returned, smiling because her catch of the day earned her some extra money. She and Pete started walking towards Lily and Alyce, and Pete asked, "Do you really think she'll be able to fix my guitar?"

"She will look at it and try her best," Song said and went on to explain that her grandmother was busy with the bride, but she surely would make time to look at his guitar.

They walked a short distance to her grandmother's store and stopped in front. Pete cautiously handed Song his guitar, and she quickly ran inside with it. While they stood outside the shop, waiting for Song to return, Pete nervously paced and thought, "What am I doing? I gave my guitar to a complete stranger." He blurted out, "I need it back A.S.A.P. to practice for the talent show."

"Don't be so negative, Pete, and besides, the talent show is over," Lily said.

Pete glared at Lily and was about to respond when Song returned. She saw that he looked extremely nervous, and she reassured him that her grandmother would have it repaired by morning.

They then noticed Song was carrying a pile of clothing. "My grandmother insisted that you attend the wedding, and she gave me some clothes for you to try on." Song led them down the street and around the corner to a tiny, white house. She told them that this was where she lived with her grandmother, since her parents died in an accident several years ago.

She invited them in to wash up and get ready for the wedding. She handed Alyce and Lily each a sundress and gave Pete a pair of tan linen pants and a blue shirt to wear. She took them to the back of the house and showed Pete where he could change. She then led the girls across the hall to her room for them to get ready.

Alyce put on a beautiful lavender sundress, embroidered with tiny white flowers. "It fits perfectly," she said as she smiled at Song. Lily twirled in front of the mirror, admiring herself in the white dress with sunflower straps.

"Not too shabby," Lily said as she spun around and glanced at herself one last time.

Song was wearing a gorgeous, emerald green dress with a sprinkling of sequins that sparkled when the light reflected off them. The color of the dress accented her beautiful, black hair and dark brown eyes. "You look gorgeous!" yelled Lily and Alyce in unison.

"Thank you. I am so nervous," Song shyly said. "I have to sing at the reception," she continued.

"Wow, I would be nervous too!" Alyce exclaimed. "That is such an honor," she continued.

"Don't worry. You're going to do great!" Lily said as she squeezed Song's hand for encouragement.

The girls found Pete waiting for them in the sitting room. He was dressed in the clothes Song had given him, and he looked very handsome. As soon as Pete saw them, he immediately asked nervously, "Any news on my guitar?"

Song just smiled and shook her head, "No."

"Are you alright, Song? You look a little nervous," Pete asked.

"I'm more than nervous. This is the first time I'm performing solo in public," Song nervously explained.

"What do you play?" Pete asked.

"Actually, I'm a singer," Song said.

"That's cool," Pete answered. "From one musical artist to another...Break a leg!"

"Wait. Why would I want to do that?" Song asked as she looked down at her legs.

The three friends laughed and explained the slang to her as they headed back to the center of town. They walked down the cobblestone road, and Song told them the history of her village. They walked through the narrow streets, and she pointed out her school, the local medical center, a church, and the market. They all looked around and enjoyed the tour.

CHAPTER 15
Wedding Bells

THE WEDDING CEREMONY WAS TAKING PLACE IN THE TOWN'S square. They could hear the chatter of the waiting guests, as they approached the crowd, and their excitement grew. Alyce took out her camera and began to take a few shots of the guests that were arriving. She noticed a large group trying to take a selfie. Alyce giggled as she watched them all try to fit in the picture. She walked over to them and offered to take the photo for them. She asked them to return the favor and take a picture of the four of them with her camera, as she called Pete, Lily, and Song over to join her.

They then weaved through the groups of people and Song led them to their seats. As soon as they sat down, they could smell the fresh flowers that were tied to the end of the aisle rows. They slid into a row towards the back, sat down and looked around in utter amazement. As they were waiting for the ceremony to begin, Song explained some of the traditional customs to the three of them.

The band played music softly in the background as the guests began to take their seats. Song's grandmother waved to them, as she joined some friends in an aisle across from where they were sitting. She looked at them smiling, happy to see the clothes she gave them, fit perfectly. Pete nudged Lily and whispered, "Do you think she has my guitar?"

"Oh yeah, Pete, she's got it in her purse," Lily said, rolling her eyes.

"Knock it off, and be quiet," Alyce whispered as she gave Lily and Pete a look.

The guests quieted down, as the ceremony was about to begin. The bride wore a beautiful light blue and gold gown. The bridal party was dressed in complementary shades of blue and tan to match the bride and groom.

They watched as the bride and groom took their places, and the ceremony began. Alyce and Lily were mesmerized by the beauty of the ceremony, and they were grateful they were able to experience the traditions of Song's culture.

The guests erupted into cheers of congratulations, as the newlyweds turned to face them. They then made their way to the reception area near the inlet by the beach. Song led them to a table and the three friends sat down. Song quickly ran off to get ready to perform. "Isn't this amazing?" Alyce asked as she looked around taking pictures. Lily and Pete looked around observing the colorful scene.

The music abruptly stopped, and the couple took their traditional seats and waved and smiled at their guests. The amazing backdrop of the sun setting into the ocean was breathtaking. Pete leaned over to Alyce and said, "Now that's a sunset!" Alyce was about to respond when Lily butted in.

"I hope the food is good. I'm starving!" Lily said, looking around at the other foodless tables.

Pete and Alyce just laughed.

Moments later, the band leader made an announcement, and everyone looked towards the dance floor. Alyce, Pete, and Lily looked around, curiously wondering what was going to happen. Lily spotted Song making her way to the microphone, and she nudged Pete and Alyce and said, "There she is."

"She doesn't look too nervous," Pete said. "Now if you want to talk about nervous…talk about leaving your guitar with a complete stranger!"

Alyce just looked at him and shook her head, as Song took the microphone in her hand.

The music began to play, and Song softly started to sing, her voice shaking a little at first. She glanced up and saw the three, quietly cheering her on, giving her the confidence she needed. Song closed her eyes and continued to sing. The song ended with a standing ovation. Pete jumped up, clapping, and yelled, "Way to go, Song!" Lily and Alyce hugged her as she joined them back at the table. They all complimented her on her singing ability, and she thanked them graciously.

"Now can we eat?" asked Lily loudly, as they all laughed.

Dinner was served, and everyone was enjoying the evening, laughing and dancing to the music of the band. Pete listened to the music and jotted some notes on a napkin. He would try them out once his guitar was repaired. Just then the music stopped, and the band leader made one last announcement. It was time to set off the lanterns on the beach. Song explained this was a custom to wish the bride and groom good luck.

They were just about to follow the other guests to the beach, when Pete began to frantically look for the notes he had been taking. "Did anyone see a napkin with some writing on it?" he asked, looking around the table. Alyce shook her head, and Song began to help Pete look for it. Pete looked at Lily, and she just looked down at the ground. "Lily! What did you do this time?" Pete growled at her.

"Sorry, Pete, the flowers were making me sneeze, and I had to blow my nose," Lily answered, as she reached into her pocket to show him the crumpled napkin with his notes smeared.

"Great! Just great! Thank you once again, Hurricane Lily," Pete said under his breath, as he sighed in defeat.

They were each given a note card and pencil to write a good luck wish for the bride and groom. Once they were finished, they folded their note cards and placed them inside a lantern. Song lit the flame, and they released it into the air. When they looked up, the beautiful lanterns lit up the night sky, like stars. Alyce took beautiful shots of the lanterns, as they floated up and drifted away. Alyce asked Pete, "What did you write?"

"Aaah just good luck, I didn't know what to say." Pete responded. "What did you write, Miss Smarty Pants?" he asked.

"I wished them a lifetime of good luck and love," Alyce answered.

"Sorry. My message wasn't so mushy gushy," Pete responded and said, "I can't wait to hear what this one wrote," while pointing at Lily.

"I wrote good luck, and on the back, I even told them they had good food at the wedding and asked if they had any leftovers," Lily answered.

"Only you, Lily." Pete said. "You do know that the lantern is not coming back, so I wouldn't count on getting any leftovers," he said.

"Oh yeah, Pete," she said, as she opened her backpack that was filled with dinner rolls and cookies. "That should get me through the night," Lily said.

Pete was just about to respond to Lily, when Song told them that it was time to go home. She and the three friends made their way to her house, completely exhausted from the day's excitement. The girls got Pete set up on the sofa, and he was already snoring by the time they headed to Song's room.

When they reached Song's room, she gave each of the girls a nightgown to sleep in. She quickly set up a roll away bed that her grandmother kept for guests. Lily jumped into Song's bed and made herself comfortable. Alyce offered to sleep on the cot, because she wasn't even sleepy yet. She didn't want to keep anyone up. The girls said goodnight to one another, and a moment later, Alyce heard Song and Lily softly sleeping. She tried to close her eyes and sleep, but her mind was racing, and she was tossing and turning. She couldn't get what was happening to them out of her mind. She got up from the bed, quietly reached into Lily's bag, and took out a sheet of paper. She sat back down on the edge of her bed and began making notes on where they had been and how many days they had been gone. She had her suspicions that they would go to whatever place they were looking at in the magazine. "The only way we will know is to test my theory," she thought to herself. She put her note inside the magazine and laid back down, after another hour of tossing and turning, Alyce finally fell asleep.

CHAPTER 16
Helping Out

AFTER A QUICK BREAKFAST, THE FRIENDS HEADED TO THE SHOP to see if Pete's guitar was ready. He anxiously paced, talking nonstop about how worried he was about his guitar. "Would it be fixed? Would it sound the same?" Pete thought to himself.

Alyce saw how concerned he was and offered him a weak smile and said, "Have a little faith, Pete," as they walked into the tiny shop. Song told them to wait, while she went into the back for a moment. Seconds later, she returned with her grandmother, who was holding Pete's guitar. She handed it to Pete and patted him on the arm. Pete examined his guitar and saw it was repaired perfectly. He gave Song's grandmother a big hug and thanked her profusely for reuniting him back with his guitar. He couldn't wait to test out the new string. Song spoke to her grandmother for a minute longer and led them around the back of the store. She explained that her family repaired old clothing for the neighboring villages and donated it for those in need. Song went on to say that she took the trip once a month, and their neighbor lent her his double peddle carriage to transport the clothes.

They helped her load the clothing into the carriage. Alyce and Lily climbed into the back seat and Pete hopped onto the peddle seat, as they waited for Song. "All I want to do is test out my new string and now I'm stuck peddling, while you two sits back and enjoy the ride," Pete complained.

"You know it wouldn't kill you to do a good deed sometime, Pete. After all, she did fix your guitar," Alyce said matter of factly.

"It's not always about you, you know," Lily teased. "Now you're my chauffeur," she continued, laughing.

Pete looked back and gave Lily a look and Lily just hushed up, knowing he was upset. Song returned, hopped onto the bike seat, and said, "After we drop off the clothes, I'll take you to see the waterfall."

Pete and Song began to peddle, and shortly, they were out of the village and riding on a dirt road. Alyce sat up, looking around at the landscape, and took a picture here and there. Lily laid back, leaned on the pile of clothing, and sketched a picture of Song performing at the wedding from one of Alyce's pictures, while Pete and Song chatted as they peddled. "Hope you have the energy for one last big hill," Song said, smiling at Pete.

"Are you kidding, Song? I can handle it," Pete said as he wiped the sweat from his brow.

He glanced at the steepness of the hill and then back at Song. He didn't want to let on that he was already exhausted and didn't think he had it in him to make it to the top.

"Let's go," Song said as she picked up the pace, forcing Pete to keep up.

"How much longer, Chauffeur?" Lily shouted as they began to peddle up the incline.

"Not now, Lily," Pete responded as he huffed loudly.

"It's just a bit further," Song assured them.

Several minutes later, they were pulling into a very small village with just one small road. Song directed Pete to a tiny doorway up ahead, and they pulled the carriage to a stop right in front. Song jumped from her seat and went inside to speak to someone.

"Anyone have some water?" Pete asked, huffing out of breath. "I'm dying over here."

Lily dug around in her backpack and pulled out a small bottle of water. "Ta Da! Lily to the rescue!" she said before she took a big sip. She then held the bottle out to Pete, and he grabbed it from her, wiping her lip gloss off the mouth of the bottle before taking a drink. "Eww gross."

"We're even now, Petey," she said laughing.

Alyce looked at the two of them and just sighed. Song returned with a young man, and he began to unload the clothing. Pete offered to help, while the girls sat on a small bench, waiting. Alyce reached over, pulled the magazine out of Lily's bag, and began looking through it. She wanted to show Song all the places they had traveled to. Alyce promptly turned to page 27, which depicted the exact scene of Song's village, and handed it to her and said, "See."

Song looked at the picture and then at Alyce. She was absolutely speechless. She wanted to know more, but first, she had to speak with Mr. Yudo about keeping an eye on the carriage. Just then, Pete rejoined them, and Song said, "I'll meet you at the bridge right over there," pointing straight ahead.

With the magazine in hand, Alyce turned to page 30, and looked at the picture, and thought to herself, "Okay, here we go. This is the big test. I guess we'll see if I am right." She stuck the magazine under her arm and walked towards the bridge ahead.

PART V
Emilio

CHAPTER 17
Across the Bridge

THEY REACHED THE BRIDGE AND SAW THAT IT WAS MADE FROM pieces of odd shaped wood, unevenly spaced and tied together with a rope. The bridge stretched over a roaring river, and the vegetation was greener on the other side. Pete looked at it and nervously said, "I don't know about this. It doesn't look too stable."

"Oh, Pete, quit it already. Song would never have told us to meet her here, if it wasn't safe," Alyce sharply said.

Alyce placed her foot onto the bridge. It swayed slightly with her weight. "Try to keep your weight even, so the bridge doesn't sway too much," she warned.   She grabbed on to the rope railing, looked back at her friends, and motioned it was safe for them to join her. The further Alyce walked, the more she felt the water, splashing up from the river below them.

"Hey, Alyce, Song said to wait at the bridge, not cross the bridge. Maybe you should come back, and wait for her," Pete said with concern.

Lily grabbed her backpack, shoved Pete out of the way, and continued after Alyce. "Let's go, Pete. See, it's safe," she said over her shoulder, as she jumped up and down to show him that the bridge was sturdy.

"Ok, Lily, quit jumping!" Alyce demanded. "I would like to make it to the other side, without going for a swim in the river under us," she continued.

Lily's jumping had caused the bridge to sway and buckle. Alyce held tighter onto the rope railing and yelled over her shoulder, "Pete will never cross the bridge if you keep it up. So quit jumping."

They saw that Pete was still on the other side, holding his newly repaired guitar. Alyce yelled across, "Come on, Pete," as she stepped off the bridge onto the other side. "Just keep your eyes straight ahead and take your time. Hold on to the railing." Pete looked down and saw the "railing" was a rope.

"Really, Alyce, you call this a railing?" Pete shouted back to her sarcastically.

"You're starting to sprout feathers," Lily responded, laughing.

"Huh?" wondered both Pete and Alyce, looking at her.

"Feathers, a chicken? Do you get it?" Lily teased, as she jumped off the last plank of the bridge onto the other side, and Alyce gave her a dirty look.

Alyce and Lily watched Pete slowly cross the bridge. The girls offered words of encouragement as he made his way. Lily noticed fog forming on the other side of the bridge near the ground. She nudged Alyce to look. Alyce turned to see what Lily wanted and saw the fog, as well. It was enveloping the other side, where they left Song, and was slowly creeping across the bridge behind Pete. The girls nervously yelled, "Hurry up, Pete. Move it," as they waved him on and pointed behind him.

Pete stopped and turned to glance behind him, and he could no longer see the land or the bridge that he crossed. The fog was thick as pea soup. He looked at Lily and Alyce with pure panic in his eyes, as he started to run. With each step he took, the bridge began to swing back and forth, with Pete almost losing his balance. "Easy Pete! You'll flip yourself off the bridge," Alyce said.

The fog was getting thicker and moving even faster. Pete took one last glance behind him and jumped the few remaining feet onto the solid ground, knocking Alyce and Lily over. Alyce's glasses went flying into a nearby bush, and the contents of Lily's backpack spilled all over the ground. Lily got up and said, "Nice landing, Pete." She went to help Alyce find her glasses. Pete was still laying on the ground and scooted himself backwards, away from the encroaching fog that was about to reach the end of the bridge. He pulled his legs backwards, just as the fog came to a slamming halt. It was like an invisible force field was protecting them. Pete sat there in complete shock for a few seconds before weakly calling out Song's name. He waited, and the only response was his own voice, echoing back towards them. "She's gone," Pete said with concern in his voice.

"Well, people seem to come and go pretty quickly around here," Lily interjected.

"People around the magazine, don't you mean? Right, Alyce?" Pete asked and got no response. He looked at Lily and shrugged his shoulders. "Alyce, where did you go?" He called out, looking around into the brush. "Oh, great. It's Alyce's turn to wander off," Pete said in frustration.

A second later, Alyce came running out. "I knew it! My experiment worked!" Alyce squealed with excitement, as she ran over to Pete and Lily.

"Experiment? What experiment are you talking about, Alyce?" Pete asked.

"I'm not your science project, Alyce. I just want to go home," Lily said sadly.

"Come on, I'll show you." Alyce answered, barely able to conceal the excitement in her voice.

They picked up their belongings and followed her into the jungle. They walked a few yards, and Alyce stopped. She turned to them and said, "Okay, let me tell you what I think is happening." Alyce went on to explain that she began to have suspicions when they arrived at Nallah's, because that page was opened randomly to a safari, just like back at Pete's house. The two listened intensely as she continued. "When we got to Song, I still wasn't sure, because that page wasn't picked on purpose. But this time, I intentionally opened the magazine to the page of the rainforest, and here we are," Alyce said, looking around.

"You did this on purpose?" Pete asked through gritted teeth. "There better be a picture of Willow Street in there, Alyce," he sternly said, as he sat down on the ground.

He began counting on his fingers and stood up and shouted, "According to my calculations, we've been gone for four days. That means it is MONDAY. The talent show is TOMORROW NIGHT! We haven't done a thing, except travel through a magazine," Pete shouted.

"Everyone must be so worried. We are missing," Lily said, and she began to sob.

Alyce gave them a moment to compose themselves, and she answered quietly, "We will figure out a way to get back home. I promise. For now, let's follow this path and see where it goes." She gave them a reassuring smile, as they followed her.

They continued deeper into the jungle and could immediately feel the temperature change. Within a few minutes, they were dripping wet from the humidity. Alyce was in the lead, with Pete and Lily close behind her. "Let's stop a minute," Alyce said, as she slowed her pace and sat down under a large palm tree.

Alyce could tell from Pete's face he was not happy. He flopped down next to Lily and angrily looked up at Alyce. "Well, Alyce, you did it this time! You wanted to do an experiment, and I appreciate your effort...but couldn't you have chosen someplace a little cooler?" he said, fanning himself with his hands.

"If whatever page you look at in the magazine somehow brings you to that place, why don't we stare at the mailing label to get home?" Lily asked.

"I guess the Amatoli house is better than nothing. At least we'll be back on Willow Street," Pete chimed in with hope in his voice.

"It's certainly worth a try," Alyce said.

The three of them gathered in a circle and stared at the address label on the magazine. Nothing happened. After a few moments, Alyce got up and said, "This is a waste of time." She adjusted her camera strap and said, "Let's go." Leading them to the path that she had discovered, they followed her deeper into the rainforest.

CHAPTER 18

Mis Amigos

ALYCE WAS WALKING A FEW FEET AHEAD, WHEN SHE CALLED back to them, "Come on, you guys! I see someone!" Pete and Lily picked up the pace.

A few yards down the path was a young boy, motioning to them, "Vamos, mis amigos. Rapido! Hurry. We are closing." He continued, "This is the last run." Alyce ran ahead of Pete and Lily and joined the young boy. Pete and Lily could see that Alyce was explaining something very quickly, and the boy nodded his head. Alyce motioned for them to come over and they ran over. She shyly introduced Pete and Lily to Emilio and smiled to herself.

Lily poked Alyce's arm and said, "Boy, is he caliente!" She held her finger up and licked it and made a sizzle sound. Alyce shot Lily a look, and Lily instantly closed her mouth. Alyce quickly introduced Emilio to them.

"¿Qué pasa, mis amigos?" he asked.

"Huh?" Pete questioned, glancing at Alyce, with a confused look on his face.

"I see someone wasn't paying attention in Spanish class," Alyce said, shaking her head.

"Yeah, Pete" Lily piped in. "You never pay attention in Spanish class. Let Alyce translate for you, so she can show off her Spanish," Lily said teasingly as she winked at Emilio.

Alyce looked down at the ground, as her face turned scarlet with embarrassment. Emilio looked at Pete, and they both just shrugged their shoulders and laughed.

Emilio took the lead, and the three friends followed behind him, while observing the topography of their latest destination. Alyce wanted to take pictures, but with the constant drizzle, she decided to wait. "Wow! This is so cool!" Lily exclaimed, as she looked around. She wished she could stop to do a sketch or two. "Hey, Amigo, do you have an umbrella, by any chance? It's a little rainy back here," she joked.

Pete lagged behind them, listening to the sounds of the rainforest. He thought, "How awesome that nature makes its own music!" He wanted to remember the sounds and somehow incorporate it into his music piece. About ten yards ahead, loomed a platform about thirty feet in the air. "What the heck is that?" Pete asked loudly.

"It's the launch platform for the zip line," Alyce replied.

"Oh, ok," Pete said. He thought for a moment and continued, "Wait. What? Who said anything about a zip line?"

Lily just looked at Pete, shook her head, and said, "Hello, Pete, where have you been?" Pete looked up at the platform and got a little queasy.

"We have to climb up there?" he quietly asked, pointing.

"Of course," answered Emilio. "How else are we going to get down from the mountain? Let's go. Who's first?" he asked.

"No way! I'm not going first!" Pete said in a determined tone, as he looked at Alyce and Lily.

"I'll go first," Alyce said as she gave Pete a look and put her foot on the first rung of the ladder and began to climb up.

"I'll go next," Lily shouted excitedly, as she ran towards Emilio. "We'll leave the chicken till the end," she called over her shoulder, as Emilio gave her a boost onto the bottom ladder rung.

Alyce was more than halfway up with Lily right behind her. Pete looked up at the platform and then at Emilio. He felt a little dizzy as he grabbed a hold of the ladder and began the climb up to the top.

"Good going, my friend! You will be okay. Take one rung at a time. Go slow, and whatever you do, don't look down," Emilio instructed, as he followed closely behind Pete.

Alyce reached the platform first and had to steady herself for a minute. The view was beautiful. The platform was just above the tree line, so you could see for miles and miles. There were beautiful, snowcapped mountains in the far distance. She could now see that there was a river below. Alyce was so captivated by the sights that she barely heard Lily asking for help as she reached the top. "Hello...a little help would be nice, Alyce!" Lily yelled to her. Alyce ran over and helped Lily over the railing. "Wow" Lily said in awe as she looked around.

Lily looked down the ladder and saw that Pete was about half way up, with Emilio close behind. "Hurry up, Pete! Wait till you see the view!" Lily shouted down to him.

"You're doing awesome, Pete. You're almost there!" Alyce said with encouragement.

"Come on, Pete, a few more steps. You can do it! But can you step on it a little? We don't have all day, you know!" Lily taunted.

The girls turned around when they heard Pete hoisting his way over the railing of the platform. Before they had the chance to help him over the railing, he had put one leg over, and his other foot got caught on the ladder rung.

Before Alyce or Lily could get to him, he lost his balance and collapsed in a sweaty heap on top of the platform. Alyce ran over to him to see if he was alright. Lily started laughing and bent over, grabbing her stomach. A second later, Emilio appeared onto the platform with them.

They sat on the platform for a few minutes, catching their breath and admiring the view. Pete wiped the sweat off his brow and asked, "What now, amigo?"

"Who's going first?" Emilio asked as he grabbed a harness for the zip line.

"I'll go, but I'll need my camera," Alyce said, raising her hand.

"I don't think you will be able to get any pictures. The zip line goes too fast," Emilio said.

"Do you mind if I take a few before we zip down?" Alyce asked.

"Si, I have to set up the harnesses for all of you," Emilio answered, and Alyce began to take a few shots.

Pete took a deep breath; he didn't care how long they sat up there. Just the thought of hanging from a wire, hundreds of feet in the air, as you zipped through a rainforest filled with all kinds of creatures, was making him nauseous. "Take all the time you need, Alyce," Pete said as he laid back on the platform, knowing that would put a few more minutes between him and his sure demise on the zip line.

As Emilio got to work, he informed them that his brother Enrique would be waiting at the bottom to assist them. He went on to explain that he and his brother helped run their family business, which consisted of a zip line and a water rafting tour. The money they make is being used to build a hospital in the town. Alyce smiled shyly at him and said, "That is such a selfless thing to do for others," Emilio smiled back at her, and she blushed and turned away.

"Ok, let's go, Alyce," Emilio said.

Alyce stood in front of Emilio as he attached her harness and pulled it tighter until it was snug fitting. He had her secure a helmet on as well. "I want to go next!" said Lily. Emilio tried the smallest harness they had on her, but it was still too big. Lily's eyes began to fill up with tears, "Then how do I get down from here?" she asked.

"Don't worry. I will take you down with me. You know, like they do when they jump out of the planes," Emilio said, as he hugged her quickly.

Pete almost turned green when he thought about sky diving. Getting through this was going to be hard enough. Emilio quickly got Pete all set with the equipment and had him stand next to Alyce. He had Lily put on the small harness, and he pulled her up and hooked her onto the front of him with her back against his chest. Next, he hooked Alyce up to the zip line, and said "Are you ready?" Alyce gave him a thumbs up, as she nervously shook her head up and down.

"Here we go," Emilio shouted as he gave her a gentle push.

Her feet left the platform, and she was off. In an instant, she began to speed up, and the trees were beginning to pass by more quickly. "Enjoy the view!" Emilio yelled as she disappeared around the bend.

Pete was next, "Are you ready?" Emilio asked him as he hooked Pete's harness onto the zip line. He could see that he looked a bit pale.

"Come on, Pete, you're killing the adventure!" Lily yelled loudly.

Emilio already had his and Lily's lines set. He saw that Pete looked extremely nervous, so he asked, "Would you rather climb back to the bottom and walk through the jungle to meet us?"

"I can do that?" Pete questioned, "Yeah. Yeah, I want to do that instead," he continued.

"Not this time, Pedro," Emilio said, laughing as he gently pushed him off the platform.

Pete, being caught off guard, felt his stomach drop instantly, and he took a gulp of air. He closed his eyes and shouted, "You lied, mi amigo. Not cool." Lily and Emilio just laughed as Pete disappeared from sight.

Last to go were Emilio and Lily. "I hope you're not afraid like your friend," he joked, looking down at her.

"Who? The flying chicken?" Lily asked.

"No comprendo." Emilio said, not understanding Lily's reference to Pete.

He then secured a lock at the top of the line, since it was almost dusk, and the zip line was closed for the day. "Do you have everything?" he asked, looking around, making sure they hadn't forgotten anything.

"Ready, Capitan," Lily responded, extending her arms out like an airplane.

Emilio pushed them off the platform, and Lily squealed with excitement, as they were off and on their way.

Alyce watched the trees go by in a blur, as she sped along faster. She laughed to herself because she could still hear Pete screaming. "Oh, brother!" she thought, rolling her eyes.

Beneath her, she could see a small stream that wound around rocks and roots of trees, finding its way to a bigger river, somewhere in the distance. She could hear all sorts of birds and other animals talking away to each other. "What an amazing ride," she thought, as she continued to zip down.

Pete kept his eyes closed and his mouth open in a perpetual scream, one hand grasping the harness and the other holding his guitar in place. A few seconds later, he opened his eyes and looked around. He finally stopped screaming long enough to see how cool everything below him looked. He took a deep breath and inhaled the warm, moist air and actually relaxed for a minute. The trees blew past him, but he could hear the sounds of the animals. He looked down and saw a monkey jumping from one tree to another. "This is unbelievable," he said out loud as he continued along.

Lily and Emilio were zooming through the air and rushing over the trees and water. She looked up and saw birds of all different colors in the trees. She commented, "I'm a bird," flapping her arms like bird wings. Emilio smiled with amusement.

Before Alyce knew it, the zip line was beginning to even out, and she began to slow down. Up ahead, she could see the landing area. Another young boy was there, waiting in a pick-up truck. As Alyce got closer, he hopped out of the truck and jogged onto the landing pad. He guided her to a gentle stop and unhooked her harness from the line. "Gracias," she said as she took her helmet off. She put out her hand and said, "Hola, I'm Alyce." Alyce looked at Enrique and asked with confusion, "Hey wait a minute. Is this some kind of joke?"

"I guess he didn't tell you we were twins," Enrique said laughing.

Alyce just looked at him shyly and smiled. He motioned for her to sit on a nearby bench to wait for the others.

Just as Pete was starting to enjoy the ride, he began to slow down. He saw he was nearing the end. He could see Alyce waiting with a boy that looked a lot like Emilio and figured that was his brother. Pete slowed to a stop on the landing area, and Enrique ran over to help him undo his harness.

"Hola," he said. "I'm Enrique, Emilio's brother. Did you enjoy the ride?"

"Yeah, it was cool. I'd do it again," Pete said, removing his helmet and shaking Enrique's hand.

"See, it wasn't that bad now, was it?" Alyce asked while she walked over and gave Pete a little shove.

"It was actually pretty awesome," Pete said as he looked at her.

The two friends gave a high five to each other as they waited for Lily and Emilio.

Lily saw lush green ferns that looked soft enough to sleep on. In just another minute, Emilio nudged her to look ahead as they began to slow. She looked and saw the landing area only a few feet ahead. Emilio guided them to a gentle stop, and Enrique helped to undo Lily's harness. "What's your name?" she asked Enrique with a shy smile.

"I am Enrique, Emilio's twin brother," he replied.

"Hey, Alyce, there's one for each of us," Lily yelled over to Alyce, and Pete threw his hands up in both frustration and embarrassment.

The two brothers secured the zip lines and put the locks on the gears. They then gathered up the harnesses and helmets and tossed them into the back of the pick-up truck, as well. Pete offered to give them a hand, but they were already done.

A moment later, they approached the truck, and Emilio told Lily, Pete, and Alyce to get in the back, as he and Enrique jumped in the front seat. Emilio started the truck and turned to the three friends and said, "We're going to tell our parents that you are tourists. We have two small cabins that we do rent out to travelers from time to time. So that way they won't be suspicious." They all nodded in unison to show they understood. Emilio shifted the truck into gear and said, "Ok, now tell us about this magazine and how you got here."

CHAPTER 19
Dinner and Dancing

"WELL, IT'S A LONG STORY, AMIGOS, AND I CAN GUARAN-tee you've never heard anything like this before," Pete said shaking his head.

"We've got a half hour ride until we are home, so let's hear it," Enrique encouraged.

"All right then, Alyce, you tell the story. It's your magazine and your experiment, so go ahead, Alyce, explain away!" Pete said, egging her on.

"Ok, fine, I will tell it!" Alyce responded to Pete in an annoyed tone.

Alyce began to explain what happened. "I found this magazine in a neighbor's driveway. The house was empty, so it was odd for there to be mail," Alyce explained.

"It wasn't exactly mail, Alyce," Lily said. "It was really trash in their driveway." She continued looking back and forth at Emilio and Enrique.

"Don't forget to tell them that they were the neighbors that disappeared without a trace," Pete interrupted.

"Am I telling the story or are you two?" Alyce said annoyed and glared at Pete and Lily. "This magazine opened up some kind of portal, I think." She hesitated for a moment, anticipating a response, but instead, the brothers glanced at each other and urged her to continue.

Just as she was about to explain what happened next, Pete not able to contain himself for a second longer, interrupted her and blurted out, "One minute, we were in my room, practicing for a talent show. Then my bedroom door led us into a field in France. A French subway dropped us off in Africa." He stopped to catch his breath and then continued. "We were climbing down a ladder in Africa and wound up in an Asian fishing village. We crossed a really freaky bridge, and now here we are, with you guys, in the middle of the rain forest," Pete finished huffing and puffing.

The two brothers looked at Pete through the back window. Pete added, "This crazy magazine is in control of where we go, but we can't figure out how to get home." He hung his head. Emilio and Enrique spoke to each other quietly, and Lily tried to listen in, with her ear pressed against the back window. Pete asked, "What are you doing?"

"Trying to hear what they're saying," she answered.

"But, Lily, you take Italian," Alyce whispered to her.

"I know, but close enough," she said and winked at Alyce.

They pulled off the road and continued up a long drive-way. At the end was a quaint home tucked away into a little clearing in the rainforest. It was made completely of stone. There was a beautiful deck that had gorgeous flowers and vines, growing around the stone pillars. All different kinds of Ivy grew up the side of the house, making it blend in to the forest scenery. It was charming.

Enrique slowed the truck to a stop. He and Emilio hopped out and hurried around the back to assist their friends out of the truck. Enrique spoke to his brother, as they all walked towards the house. All Alyce could get out of the conversation was that Enrique told Emilio to hurry. Enrique continued walking towards the direction of the house, while Emilio led them up a small path. Emilio said, "Remember you are tourists that came for zip lining and water rafting. Enrique will tell my parents that we have guests, and I will show you to your cabins."

"We hope we're not being an inconvenience," Alyce said, slightly concerned.

"No, no problema. My mom will be fine. She loves to entertain guests," Emilio said with a smile.

A moment later, they reached a little wooden bridge that crossed a small, slow, babbling stream. On the other side of the bridge was a tiny wooden cabin with a blue door and small porch with two bamboo chairs. "It's so cute!" Lily shouted as she ran across the narrow bridge.

"Obviously this is where you girls will be sleeping," he said, laughing. "Please let me know if you need anything." Alyce thanked Emilio and hurried across the bridge to meet Lily.

The girls opened the door, and Lily ran in and hopped on the one small bed. "I could really use a nap right about now," Lily said as she yawned.

"Come on! Get up, Lazy Bones! Wash your face and fix that crazy looking hair of yours," Alyce said in a scolding tone.

Lily stuck her tongue at Alyce and sat up. She rummaged through her backpack and found one of her lipsticks and immediately began applying a thick coat. Alyce shook her head and said, "We're not going to Broadway, Lily. Lighten up on the lips." Lily stuck her tongue at Alyce again, as she wiped the lipstick off on a napkin she pulled out of her bag.

Emilio and Pete continued up the path a bit further and stopped at another small bridge. On the other side was an identical cabin, except this one had a red door. Emilio motioned for Pete to go across. For a second Pete got a little queasy, but then he remembered he just zip lined, so he looked forward and walked across without being nervous. "I think I've conquered my fear of heights," he said to himself out loud, as he stepped off the bridge and onto the cabin's little porch. He looked back at Emilio and gave him a thumbs up. Pete went inside and looked around, "Pretty cool. At least I'll get a decent night's sleep tonight." He felt the bed and said, "That'll do." He washed his face and combed his hair, slung his guitar around his back and headed out the door. He crossed the bridge, looked down the path, and saw that Emilio was already there waiting, and he hurried down to meet him.

The girls quickly got ready for dinner. Alyce took her camera, and Lily took her sketch pad and charcoal pencil. They walked across the little bridge and towards the house. They saw that Pete and Emilio were already waiting for them at the bottom of the steps leading to the house.

As they walked up the stone path to meet up with the boys, they noticed everyone was there, but Enrique. Emilio explained that his brother was letting their mother know they have guests in the cabins tonight. He guided Pete, Alyce and Lily around to the backyard, and told them that they usually have dinner out on the patio together. "Come on. I'll introduce you to our mother," Emilio said smiling.

"Before we meet your family, maybe we should know where we are." Alyce said stopping short, with Pete and Lily shaking their heads in agreement.

"Yeah, Amigo, where are we?" Pete asked.

"You are in Colombia," Emilio answered.

"Colombia?" The three friends answered in unison.

"Yes, Colombia," Emilio repeated and continued. "Where did you think you were?" he asked.

"Well, about four hours ago, we were in Thailand, and now..." Pete began explaining, but Alyce had cut him off.

"Let's go meet your mom," Alyce said, giving Pete an elbow to his side.

They walked up the few steps to the patio and could see that the table was set beautifully. There was a fresh flower centerpiece and several white candles scattered across the table. It looked warm and inviting. They could hear music playing softly in the background as they approached the table. On the other side of the patio, there was a small fire pit, adding to the welcoming environment.

Moments later, Enrique appeared, carrying a plate of rice and chicken. Emilio followed him with several other bowls and platters. Lily took a deep whiff of the delicious smelling food, and her stomach grumbled so loud that Alyce had to try to cover the sound with a fake cough, as she looked at Lily. "I'm starving. What can I say?" Lily responded. Pete, Alyce, and the two brothers just looked at Lily and laughed.

Suddenly, they heard a woman's voice, "What's so funny?" she asked as she walked towards them, carrying a water pitcher and placing it on the table. She smiled at them and said, "Welcome to our home. I am Carol, and my husband is Armando Vivas. He should be joining us any minute," she continued. "Please call me Carol," she said after Emilio introduced their new friends.

He explained to his mother that they were on a tour and already did the zip line today and will do the rafting tomorrow. She nodded at them and said, "I hope you enjoyed the zip line, and the river should be beautiful tomorrow. Please take a seat. Everything is ready."

As soon as they were seated, they began passing around bowls and dishes of delicious smelling foods and putting a spoonful of this and piece of that onto their plates. Lily had her plate piled high with a bit of everything. Alyce gave her a stern look, and Lily replied, "What? I'm hungry, and besides, I want to be a little worldly and try new things." The group just smiled and laughed, as they too began to eat.

Several minutes later, a handsome man came out from the back doors of the house. "Siempre...I'm late," he said.

"Hola Papi," the boys said together.

"We have guests tonight," Emilio told him.

"Ahh, great! I am Armando Vivas," the boy's dad said as he introduced himself to the three friends.

He immediately joined them at the table and made himself a plate. Enrique and Emilio's parents explained what they did for a living. Carol worked in the local school teaching English to the students. Armando was a holistic doctor that traveled from village to village on a weekly basis to treat patients. The boys were actually the ones that decided to try to raise money to help with the construction of the new hospital. They came up with the idea of the zip line and the rafting trips. That way they were also giving the tourists a fun experience.

After the meal, the girls helped Carol clean up quickly and returned outside. Armando had lit the fire pit and was sitting and talking with Pete. Alyce and Lily joined them, along with Carol, who carried a tray with some fresh fruit for dessert. Suddenly Enrique and Emilio appeared with a trumpet, a small guitar and traditional Guitarrón, which Emilio handed to his father. Pete was happy to see the others bringing out instruments. He was hoping to get some local inspiration. The group just sat and listened as the three began to play. Emilio encouraged Pete to join in. Pete picked up his guitar and followed the music. He mentally made a few notes here and there, as he continued to play along. Before long, Carol was up on her feet and dancing. She pulled the girls up and began to teach them some basic dance steps, and they followed along easily. They played music all evening, laughing, and dancing. Carol even got Pete to do a few steps with her. "I think this has been my favorite night of all" Alyce said as she and Lily continued to dance along with the others. She asked Mr. Vivas to take a picture of them all. He did, and then, the parents shooed them off to bed, because they were getting up early to do the rafting trip.

They thanked Armando and Carol for a wonderful night, and Enrique and Emilio brought their new friends back to their cabins. Pete was thrilled to have a bed all to himself, so that he could finally get a good night's sleep. As soon as his head hit the pillow, he was softly snoring, and it wasn't long before they were all sleeping soundly, with the symphony of the jungle around them.

CHAPTER 20

Down the River

Lily was stirred from her sleep by a bird chirping in the window. She sat up, stretched, and hopped out of bed. Alyce was still asleep, and she could tell from the lighting that it was still early. She grabbed her sketch pad, went out on the little deck, and sat in one of the chairs. She looked around, trying to decide what to draw first. She was working on a beautiful colored bird that sat on a tree limb across the little creek. Alyce startled her as she stepped out on to the deck and the bird quickly flew off. Lily looked at Alyce and just huffed. "Well, good morning to you, too!" Alyce replied.

"I was right in the middle of a sketch, and you scared my subject away." Lily said angrily.

"Oh, I'm sorry, Lily. I really am. I didn't know you were working out here," Alyce said apologetically.

Before Alyce sat down next to Lily, she took her cell phone from her back pocket and placed it on a small table next to them. She noticed that her phone battery was very low and hoped that Emilio had a charger that she could use before they left to go rafting.

Unexpectedly, they heard a call from across the bridge. It was Emilio. "Buenos Dias Mis Amigas," he said loudly.

"Buenos Dias," Alyce replied waving at him.

"We'll be right there," Lily said. "We just have to grab our stuff."

"No problem. I'm going to make sure Pedro is awake. It's almost time to go," Emilio responded.

Emilio reached the bridge leading to Pete's cabin. Before he had a chance to speak, Pete stuck his head out of the door and said, "Morning, Amigo."

"Pedro, get your stuff. It's almost time to go," Emilio said. He turned and began jogging back towards the house and shouted, "Meet us on the back patio."

Pete grabbed his guitar and sheet music, looked back inside the cabin, and said out loud, "Thanks for the first good night's sleep in a week," and he gave a high five to the bed. He left the cabin and ran across the bridge. He waved to Alyce and Lily as he approached their cabin.

The girls hurried across to meet up with Pete. The three friends walked towards the house where Emilio and Enrique were waiting for them. Their mother had made a quick breakfast for them before leaving for work. The table had tons of fruit, small pastries and breads, and fresh squeezed orange juice. There was a plate of fried plantains and homemade yogurt, too.

While they ate breakfast, Enrique explained that he was working the zip line today and that Emilio was running the rafting trips. They switched so that Emilio could take them on the first ride of the day. He went on to explain that first, they had to drive him and the gear up to the zip line starting point.

Once they all finished breakfast, they grabbed their things and headed towards the waiting truck. Alyce didn't have a chance to ask Emilio for his phone charger, because they were in a hurry to drop off the gear.

Emilio jumped in the driver's seat and invited the two girls to sit in the front with him because it was a rough ride up to the platform. Enrique opened the passenger side door of the truck, and Lily hoisted herself up immediately and scooted right next to Emilio. She turned towards Alyce and playfully stuck out her tongue. Alyce shook her head and climbed in after Lily, without comment. Enrique closed their door and told them to hold on tightly. Enrique and Pete jumped into the back of the truck and were on their way.

Emilio backed out from the house, quickly put the truck into gear, and sped off onto a tiny rocky dirt path. "Girls, hold on. It's about to get a little rough," Emilio said. The girls nervously held on and tried to give a weak smile in response. As the road became more and more uneven, Emilio accelerated, and Enrique warned Pete to hold on.

As they drove deeper into the rainforest, the terrain became so uneven, that Pete almost bounced out of the truck bed.

"I told you to hold on, Pedro," Enrique said laughing.

Pete held onto the side of the truck with both of his hands, bouncing and waiting for this ride to end.

Emilio slowed down and put the truck into park as they reached the bottom of the zip line. He told the girls to wait there, as he jumped out to help his brother unload the gear. Enrique and Pete stood up in the back of the truck and began passing the equipment to Emilio, who laid it onto the ground. Once they had unloaded the gear, Enrique and Pete jumped out of the truck and Enrique expertly climbed the ladder up to the platform. He threw down a cord with a clamp to attach the harnesses and helmets. Emilio grabbed hold of the line and Pete started passing him the equipment, so he could latch them onto the cord that Enrique had sent down. Emilio yelled up to Enrique when he was done, and Enrique began to hoist up the equipment.

Once his brother was set, Emilio got back into the truck, with the girls still in the front seat, and instructed Pete to get into the back. "Oh, man, again," Pete said.

"The way down is much smoother," Emilio assured. "One more stop to unlock the line for Enrique, and we are off," he continued.

After unlocking the zip line, they drove the short ride to the river bank. Emilio explained to Lily, Pete and Alyce that his father had invited them to come tour the hospital after their rafting ride. They were all excited to see the work being done on the hospital. Emilio parked the truck, and they all jumped out and followed him towards the river. Emilio walked towards a small wooden building and opened the lock on the door. He began pulling large inflated tubes out and Pete ran over to help him lug them to the edge of the water. Emilio took a rope, quickly tied all the tubes together, and double checked to make sure they were secured. He then made one last trip to get the life jackets. Lily burst out and said, "I thought we were going rafting, not rubber tubing!"

"Where's your sense of adventure, Miss Worldly?" Pete asked sarcastically.

Lily made a face at Pete and was about to respond, when Emilio returned with life jackets, helmets and a small tarp.

As he handed out the equipment, he instructed them to put on their jackets securely and to fasten their helmets.

Alyce slipped her phone inside of a pocket in her life vest, in hopes of keeping it from getting wet. Emilio wrapped Pete's guitar and Lily's bag in a small tarp and tied it down onto the empty tire. "Thanks Emilio, I was worried about my guitar getting wet," Pete said.

"Worried about your guitar? All my prized possessions are in my bag, and I can't afford to get them wet," Lily said.

"No problemo, mis amigos," Emilio reassured them that their belongings were safe.

Once they were all ready, Emilio took Alyce's hand and led her to the raft. She gulped as she looked back and forth from the tubes to the three of them.

Emilio assured Alyce that the raft was safe, as she took her seat. He secured a rope across her lap and gave her a reassuring smile. Next, he helped Pete onto his tube on the other side of Alyce to balance out the weight. Lastly, he took Lily by the hand and had her sit in the center tube. He pulled the rope extra tight because he was afraid if they hit rough water, she might bounce right out of the tube.

Emilio made sure they had their helmets fastened and checked their ropes one last time. "Ok, Amigos, here we go!" Emilio said, as he waded in the water and pushed the raft into the gently flowing river. Once the water was up to his waist, he jumped up on the tubes, using a large stick to push them along. Emilio explained how the river appeared to change colors at certain times of the year.

He went on to say that the pink and green shades were due to the algae that grew in the water. "I think there are a few patches up ahead," Emilio said pointing.

Lily squeezed Alyce's hand as the raft caught the current and began to move more quickly down the river. Pete looked around nervously and pulled at the ropes to make sure they were tied tightly. Alyce looked at them both and said, "Would you two calm down and just enjoy the ride!"

Lily relaxed a bit and looked around. "Wow, this is really beautiful," she commented as she pushed her helmet back, so she could get a better view.

Pete checked the rope that was holding down his guitar, and made sure it was still secured tight in the small tarp Emilio had wrapped it in. He took a deep breath, and finally started to enjoy the sights and sounds around them as they floated slowly along.

"Look up ahead," Emilio said excitedly. "There, on the left, is a patch of pink algae." The three friends all leaned over to see the incredible sight.

"Look," Lily shouted, "it's green up there."

"Darn it!" Alyce said dismayed, "I can't even get a picture of this! My camera is inside of Lily's bag." So, she did not even attempt to reach for it.

"Forget about taking a picture!" Lily shouted.

Alyce looked up and saw them quickly approaching some rapids. She looked nervously at Emilio. He just smiled at the group and said, "Hold on, my friends!"

Pete looked over his shoulder and saw they were heading right into the wild waves of the river. There were huge rocks and boulders on both sides of them, and even smaller ones that needed to be maneuvered around. The cold water began to splash all over them. They picked up speed, as the tube began to merge into another branch of the river. They flowed with the rapid current and were soon dipping and rising with the flow of the water. Lily grabbed Alyce's hand again and shouted over the raging sound of the water, "This is so much fun!"

Just as Pete was about to respond, a big wave came over the side of the tube and soaked Lily completely. Pete and Alyce looked at her and laughed. She looked at them angrily and spit out a mouthful of water.

Emilio turned to the three friends and said, "Hold on. The river is much higher than I thought." Emilio worked his way around the edge of the tubes, pushing them off huge rocks, sometimes having to jump into the water to steer them back into the flowing river. As they rounded the bend, they could see that the water was getting rougher as they were approaching the fork in the river up ahead. Alyce looked at Emilio nervously, as he pushed them away from another patch of boulders.

"Which way do we go?" asked Pete, as he held on to the rope with one hand, using the other to keep Lily from falling off. "This is not fun at all!" Pete shouted.

"Ok, amigos, we need to go down the right branch of the river, so everybody lean to the right and hang on," Emilio instructed.

The makeshift raft got caught up in the quickly moving current of the raging rapids. Emilio gave them a good push off the rocks to propel them into the right direction of the fork in the river. Suddenly, a fast-moving rush of water side swiped the raft and pushed them into the opposite direction. As a last resort, Emilio jumped into the water and used a large stick to push them off a rock to try to redirect them once again. Before he could climb back onto the tubes it was hit with the next wave and the raft went spinning out of control towards the left, leaving Emilio standing on the rock, as the three friends continued to rush down the river.

Pete looked around in a panic when he realized that Emilio was no longer on the raft, and they were by themselves. Emilio was standing in waist high water, waving at them wildly. Lily shouted "Adios, Emilio. We'll see you at the end of the ride," as she waved back to him.

"I don't think he was saying goodbye" Pete shouted nervously. "I think he was warning us!"

"Warning us about what?" Lily asked.

Pete and Lily looked around as Alyce said, "Warning us about that!!!" As she pointed straight ahead, Pete and

Lily looked in the direction that she was pointing in, and Lily started screaming.

"Untie the ropes," Alyce shouted, "or we'll be dragged down and crushed by the tubes."

"Undo the tubes? How will we go down without the tubes?" Pete asked.

"We're going to have to cut these two tubes loose and let them go over the falls first," Alyce explained.

"If we cut them loose, that means my guitar is going to go with it," Pete frantically said.

"It's either that, or we get tangled in the lines and we drown," Alyce shouted.

Pete quickly freed himself from the ropes that were tied across his lap, while he glanced up quickly and saw they were rapidly approaching the falls. He then untied Lily and held on to her hand. Alyce untied herself, and cautiously stood on top of the tube. She grabbed on to Lily's hand trying to keep her balance. She was screaming something over the roaring of the water, as they approached the waterfall ahead. It was to no avail. They could not hear her. She waved her arms, got their attention, and motioned for them to stand up and let the tubes go over.

Pete followed Alyce's lead and stood carefully balancing himself on the edge of his tube. Pete grabbed Lily's other hand, as they rushed toward the falls. "I just want you guys to know I love you!" Pete shouted.

"I stole two cupcakes that your aunt made for the school party," Lily confessed, near tears.

"Oh, would you two stop it. We're about to go over a waterfall, and you're talking about stolen cupcakes? Really, I think we have a bigger problem," Alyce said, as she pointed to the edge of the waterfall.

"Once the tubes go over, we have to try to dive out as far as we can. When you go under, paddle as hard as you can to the surface and away from the falling water," Alyce instructed loudly.

"Wait, I don't know how to dive! I don't even know how to swim," Lily yelled.

"You got to be kidding me," Pete responded.

"How'd I know we'd be diving off of a waterfall?" Lily asked sarcastically.

"Get on my back, and wrap your arms around my neck, and whatever you do, don't let go," Pete said panicking, as he scooped up Lily and threw her on his back.

"This would have been the winning shot, right, Alyce?" Pete asked sarcastically.

Alyce ignored him and said, "Okay, here we go. Take a deep breath, and on the count of three, remember to dive out as far as you can and kick for the surface."

She looked at Pete and Lily, smiled nervously, and gave them a thumbs up. They all took a breath and followed Alyce as she dove from the top of the falls.

Alyce hit the water first with a slap, and she was immediately pushed under. She swam away from the pouring waterfall and paddled to the surface, with all her might. As she popped up, she took a deep breath and scanned the area for Pete and Lily. She saw Pete struggling to stay afloat about six feet from her. He was flailing his arms around wildly, trying to keep his head above water. Lily was frantic, trying to climb on top of him which was forcing him back under the water.

"Lily! Stop panicking! You're going to drown him!" Alyce yelled, as she rapidly swam over to help them.

Alyce grabbed a hold of Lily's arm and used her other arm to get them into shallower water. "Lily! Keep your head up and start kicking your feet as hard as you can! I'm trying to get us to the shore," Alyce exclaimed, as she swam as hard as she could away from the waterfall. Lily held onto Alyce with all her might and kicked her feet like Alyce told her.

Pete paddled furiously down the river a few feet to try to catch the tubes, but to no avail, they were out of reach.

By that time Alyce and Lily had reached the riverbank. They collapsed on the sandy shore and watched as Pete bobbed up and down in defeat, as he watched the tubes get pushed further down the river.

"Forget it, Pete. We can't catch them," Alyce yelled as he swam back towards them.

"It's gone. It's all gone," he said as he crawled dismally back towards Lily and Alyce. He collapsed in an exhausted heap on the sand.

Alyce stood on the bank of the river and looked around. The raft had floated out of sight, with all their belongings. She couldn't believe it. "My camera and pictures, and the magazine! Her sketches and your guitar, are gone!" Alyce explained in dismay, as she took off her life jacket and helmet.

"Now what are we going to do?" Alyce wondered, as she pulled out her phone, to find it was now soaking wet. It was ruined! "Oh, just great!" Alyce thought as she shoved it into her back pocket.

"All our hard work is floating down the river," Lily said sadly.

"My guitar is gone. G.O.N.E. Gone!" Pete shouted to no one in particular.

"All of our stuff is G.O.N.E. Gone! Pete!" Lily yelled back at him, as they began to argue.

Alyce just closed her eyes for a minute, took a deep breath got up and started walking away from them. She needed to block out the chatter of Pete and Lily going back and forth.

Pete and Lily were too busy arguing to notice that Alyce had gotten up and wandered away. Alyce sat down for a moment and almost started to cry. "How are we going to ever get home?" she whispered to herself. She looked up and saw an opening in the rocks. It looked like a doorway that had been carved by water flowing for about a million years. Alyce slowly walked a little closer to investigate. She easily climbed the few rock steps to the threshold of the formation. "Could it be possible?" she asked out loud to herself. "Only one way to find out," she thought, as she stepped through the water carved doorway.

PART VI
The Chief

CHAPTER 21

Gateway to The Forest

ALYCE IMMEDIATELY FELT THE TEMPERATURE CHANGE, AND SHE took a breath of the fresh air. The trees had turned from palm trees and rainforest overgrowth to a forest of fresh smelling pine trees. The air felt much cooler. Alyce walked for a moment or two and sat down on a nearby rock. She pulled out her phone, only to discover that it was dead. She began to cry out of frustration. She thought for sure this would be the way home, but it wasn't. She looked around and thought, "Not only am I lost, but my two best friends could be stuck inside of a magazine." She covered her face with her hands and began to sob. She realized that they may never get home. She heard someone approaching and looked up, startled to see a young boy standing in front of her.

"Are you ok?" he asked.

"Yes, yes. I'm okay," she answered, holding back a sob, looking around to see where the boy may have come from.

Through her tears, Alyce explained that her two friends were stuck on the other side of the rock formation. "They will find their way. Don't worry," he assured her, with a slight smile.

Thirty seconds later, Pete and Lily came bursting through the passageway that Alyce had just come through. Lily was insistently saying, "Pete, I told you this is the way she went," pointing straight ahead.

"I'm not trusting your directions after this experience," Pete said, stopping short as he felt the immediate temperature change.

He looked at Lily and threw his arms up in frustration. "Well, where the heck are we now?" he asked, while spinning in a circle, looking around. Alyce and the young boy turned when they heard the ruckus behind them.

"I think your friends are here," the boy said with a wide smile.

Alyce turned and saw Lily and Pete heading towards them through the trees. She jumped up and ran over and hugged each of them. "I never thought I would see you guys again," she said, as she hugged them again. "Come with me. There's somebody over here that we need to talk to, she said, dragging Pete and Lily each by their hands.

"Oh! Great, Alyce. Where did you bring us now?" Pete questioned angrily.

"Just follow me, Pete," she said as she led them back towards the young boy that she had been speaking to.

"There is no more magazine to travel through, Alyce," Pete continued.

They saw the young boy patiently waiting sitting on a log, whittling something out of wood. As they approached him, he looked up, smiled, and said, "I'm Sam."

After they introduced themselves, Sam asked, "How did you find your way here?"

Pete looked at Sam and then at Alyce and said, "Do you want to do the honors? I don't have the energy."

"Okay. This is what happened, and this is how it started," Alyce began explaining.

"You two had a turn telling the story. It's my turn. You better sit down for this, Sam," Lily demanded.

Sam looked at her oddly because he was already sitting. Pete and Alyce joined Sam, sat down next to him, and waited attentively for Lily to begin. Lily began telling the story, "Are you ready for this?" she asked, pacing back and forth in front of them, now eye level to them while they sat. She took a deep breath and began. "On the way home from school, six days ago," she said with her eyes popping out, looking at Alyce. She continued, "Alyce picked up the neighbor's trash, which was some

154

wacky magazine. I'll get to that part. Fast forward, we're now in Pete's room, and he is ragging on us about some dumb talent show that he didn't even sign us up for. Take a bow for that major oversight," she said, glancing at Pete while she took another deep breath. "Alyce started flipping through that magazine she found, and that's when it all started. We walked through a doorway and wound up in France and had the most delicious French pastries and the best vanilla milkshake I ever had," Lily proudly said. "We missed the train with no fault of my own and wound up in Africa, where we saw elephants and chased poachers. Alyce takes out that magazine again, and it turns out whatever page we are looking at, that's where we go...yeah yeah yeah! Next, Mr. Rockstar over here breaks his guitar. The good thing about that was we were invited to a wedding, where we ate delicious food. Then Alyce did her secret experiment on us, and we wound up on a zipline and then on a raft, where we almost died going over a waterfall. Thank you, Alyce, by the way," Lily said, while making a face at her, and then continued, "We somehow make it over the falls alive, only to find all of our work slowly floating down the river. After dragging ourselves on shore, half-drowned, may I tell you, then we look up, and Alyce, our tour director, is gone! Fast forward... Here we are!" Lily finished. "Ta da" she said and took a bow. The three of them sat with their mouths agape, just starring at Lily after that depiction of their adventure.

"So, basically, it's Alyce's fault," Pete said looking at Sam.

Before Alyce could respond, Sam said, "I think you should follow me home. There is someone there that might be able to help you." They looked at one another and shook their heads "Yes" in agreement, as Sam began to lead the way.

They followed Sam in silence, completely defeated by the loss of their hard work. "I guess we can kiss the talent show goodbye," Pete sadly said.

"I think getting home is a little more important that your talent show, Pete," Alyce said, getting annoyed with his selfishness.

"It's not all about your talent show, Pete," Lily added.

They continued walking without further commenting. Suddenly, it dawned on Pete that they had no way back to Willow Street. He ran up to Alyce who was a few yards in front of him and asked, "Any ideas as to how we'll get home, Genius?"

Alyce did not comment and continued to follow Sam. "Where are we going?" whispered Lily to Alyce.

"I think he's taking us to his house. He said there was...." Alyce whispered back as Pete interrupted.

"Do you two realize that we have no way of getting home? You know home, you do remember that place, don't you?" Pete asked, loudly whispering, following Sam.

"We have no other choice at this point. We have to trust Sam," Alyce said.

Sam stopped at the edge of a large clearing and pointed to the small village ahead. "Come on," he said, "If anyone can help you, it will be Chief Neolin."

"I've never met a chief before," Lily said looking up, grabbing Alyce's hand.

"Do you think any of us have?" Pete asked while he turned to look at Lily.

"Would you two stop it already!" Alyce hissed at them.

Sam led them into the center of the tiny town. "Wait here, I'll be right back," he said.

The three friends looked around and observed their surroundings. A few women were gathered around an open fire, cooking something in a few pots and roasting some meat. A few others were grinding some grains to be used to make bread. The wind blew gently in their direction, and the smell of the cooking food made their stomachs rumble. Pete looked at Lily and said, "I know, I know, you're starving, right?" Lily and Alyce just giggled as they waited for Sam to return.

Sam came running over to them and said, "Follow me. The Chief wants to meet you." Alyce and Pete looked at each other, and Lily grabbed both of their hands. Sam could see that they were all nervous. "Don't worry. Chief Neolin is a very kind and wise man. If anyone can help you, it will be him," he reassured them. The three friends didn't want to get their hopes up, but they tried to remain positive.

They slowly approached a large white teepee, and Sam announced their arrival and flipped open the flap. He motioned for them to go inside and sit down across from the chief. They sat down and looked up at the Chief. "I'm Chief Neolin," he said, introducing himself. He had a kind face with deep wrinkles in his dark tanned skin. He had his salt and pepper hair pulled back into two braids and was wearing a necklace that had different animal teeth hanging on it, with a large bear claw dangling from the center. He looked up at the three friends and smiled slightly, his green eyes sparkling as he spoke, "Please tell me about your journey."

Pete, Lily and Alyce introduced themselves, explained what had happened, and told him all about the places they had visited. They went on to tell him about the new friends they had made along the way. When they had finished telling their tale to the Chief, Pete added quietly, "We lost everything. It all washed down the river."

"Even the magazine, it was our only hope of getting home," Alyce said with a sigh.

The Chief listened intently to their story, and when they finished, he sat silently with his eyes closed. The three friends just stared at him in silence. A moment later, he opened his eyes and addressed them, "May I ask you a few questions?"

The friends looked at each other and then back at the Chief. "Sure, Mr. Chief," said Lily. Alyce poked her in the side and shot her a look to be quiet.

"Of course, you may," Alyce answered him.

"Tell me what you learned about all the different people along your journey," the Chief asked.

"They were kind to everyone and accepted us without question," Pete said shyly.

"They were compassionate to others in the work they did," Alyce responded.

"They love and protect the elephants," Lily said giggling.

"They all helped others and believe their work makes a difference," Alyce said as she looked right at the Chief.

He sat for a moment, smiled at them, and said, "I think you have learned much from your new friends and that you can use the things you've learned in the future. You must always have faith and believe that anything is possible."

The Chief invited them to join the tribe for their evening meal, so Sam led them back to the center of their little camp. "It's about time we get to eat," Lily whispered to Alyce, as they joined the others and shared a delicious meal with them.

Sam told stories of the history and traditions of the tribe and of the great Chiefs that had led them through the years. Lily began to yawn, and she suddenly felt sad. She missed home, she missed her mom, and she even missed her pesty brother. Pete only picked at his dinner, having no appetite after losing his guitar and his music.

Alyce looked at Sam sadly and said "I think we've had a long day. Would it be okay if we went to rest?" Sam nodded and began to get up from the table.

"I will take them," The Chief said motioning for Sam to sit back down.

Alyce, Pete, and Lily got up from the table and said goodnight to Sam and the other villagers. The Chief took a lantern and began to lead the way, and the friends followed him sleepily. Just then, a little girl not much older than five or six came running behind them. She ran up to the Chief and grabbed his hand. He looked down smiled at her and said something that they could not hear. The Chief suddenly stopped in front of a large teepee. He turned to them and said, "Always believe that you can overcome any obstacle in your path. You must have faith that everything will work out as it should. Now go inside, and get some rest. Tomorrow you will know what to do." As the Chief was speaking, the little girl was hiding behind him, peeking out and smiling at Lily. Lily gave her a little wave, and the girl smiled widely.

The Chief opened the flap, and Alyce and Pete said goodnight and stepped inside. The little girl ran over to Lily, just as she was about to close the flap of the teepee, and she handed her a small, white dream catcher. It was beautiful. Lily gave her a quick hug, and off she went, running behind the Chief.

CHAPTER 22

Blank Pages

PETE SAT DOWN ON ONE OF THE COTS AND RUBBED HIS HAND across a soft wool blanket that covered it. "Now this is comfortable" he said, as he stretched out on the cot. He fluffed up the feather pillow and put his head down. He was exhausted. Lily hopped onto one of the other cots and examined the little dream catcher. It was made with all white feathers, and it almost seemed to sparkle. She twirled it around on the string, watching the iridescent colors spin around and around, as her eyes began to close. It wasn't long before she was softly snoring, with the dream catch tucked under her pillow.

Alyce just sat on the cot and was deep in thought when Pete asked, "What is it, Alyce? Why do you look so worried?" Alyce looked over at Pete and crossed the teepee to sit next to him. She didn't want to wake Lily. Pete moved over on his cot and said, "Boy, this must be serious." Alyce looked at him and sat down.

"I know we've been talking and even making jokes about the magazine," she whispered. "Pete, we all know that, in some crazy way, it was the magazine that started this whole journey, and somehow, we've been trans- ported to every place in the magazine. But I think we have a real problem now."

"Are you worried because we lost the magazine?" Pete asked, looking at her with concern.

"No, I'm concerned because there were no other pictures in the magazine. After the rainforest, the next page was blank," she responded.

"Blank?" he questioned.

"Blank," Alyce said.

"Don't freak me out now, Alyce," Pete said nervously. "Let's just go to sleep like the Chief said. He seems like a smart guy. Maybe by tomorrow, he will have come up with a solution," he said, trying to reassure her.

Alyce took a deep breath and walked back over to her cot and said "You're right. It's been a long day, and we all need to get a good night's sleep." She laid down and closed her eyes. "Good night, Pete," she said sleepily.

"Good night, Alyce," he responded as he drifted off to sleep.

PART VII

Address Unknown

CHAPTER 23
Where Are We Now?

PETE WOKE UP SUDDENLY TO THE SOUND OF A BIRD SQUAWK-
ing. "What now?" he thought to himself, as he rolled over
and slowly opened his eyes. He looked up, rubbed his
eyes, and looked again. He sat up and looked at the
clock 5:49pm. "Holy cow, what a dream I just had!" he
said to himself as he gently slapped his cheeks to wake
himself up. "Look at these two," he mumbled to himself. Alyce and Lily were sprawled across the floor, sound
asleep. "Hey, wake up, you two," Pete said as he shook
Alyce's shoulder.

"Wait? Where are we?" Alyce mumbled, still half
asleep.

Pete snapped his fingers in front of her face, and her eyes opened wide. "What's wrong with you?" she snapped at him "I was having the craziest dream," she said as she stood up and stretched herself.

"Wait," Pete said. "What did you dream about? Because I had a crazy dream too!"

Alyce nudged Lily to wake up. Lily just sighed and rolled over, leaving a white, feathered dream catcher on a pillow. Pete and Alyce looked at each other when they both saw it. "No way!" he said.

"Where did that come from?" Alyce asked.

A moment later, they heard Lily talking in her sleep. "Oui, oui, Dreamy. Wait for me!" Pete and Alyce looked at each other and back at Lily.

"Could it be? Did we all dream the same dream?" Pete asked Alyce suspiciously.

"Only one way to find out. Let's wake this one up," Alyce answered.

Alyce tried to shake Lily awake, but she only rolled over, still snoring. Pete bent down and yelled in her ear, "Buenos Dias, Amiga." Lily sat up, rubbing her head. "That wasn't very nice," she said, as Pete and Alyce burst out into laughter.

"What were you dreaming about Lily, and why were you speaking French in your sleep?" Pete asked her with curiosity.

"A dream? I was in France, you dummy, and so were you guys," Lily said, looking at them in confusion.

"Did we see elephants with painted tusks by any chance?" Alyce asked.

"Of course, we did, and then we went to a wedding. What's wrong with you guys?" she asked, growing even more annoyed.

"Did we go ziplining?" Pete asked.

"DUH! Pete you were the biggest chicken of them all. I'm glad you're starting to remember now," Lily said, trying to fix her bed head.

"It better of been a dream," Pete said.

"I don't think so," Lily said, dangling the dream catcher in front of them.

"Don't you guys remember Chief Neolin putting us in the teepee to go to sleep? Are you sure you guys didn't bump your heads somewhere?" Lily seriously asked.

Pete turned towards his guitar stand and saw that there was nothing there. He hurried over to the empty stand while frantically searching his pockets for his music sheets. They were gone too! Pete began yelling, "No, no, no, no! This can't be happening."

"What? What's wrong?" Alyce asked.

"Alyce, where is your camera?" Pete asked.

"What are you talking about Pete? It's right there on your desk" She said pointing at the now empty spot where her camera had been sitting.

"No, no, no, no, no! This can't be happening!" Alyce said, running over to the desk.

"Yes, yes, yes, yes, yes! It all went floating down the river: the guitar, the camera, my backpack, and that magazine too. They're all gone," Lily responded. "How do you guys not remember that?" she asked, looking at them.

"We remember. We remember. I was hoping it was a dream, but now I see it was a nightmare!" Pete exclaimed as he looked all over, ransacking his drawers and closet for any shreds of his beloved guitar.

Lily and Alyce joined in, even extending their hunt into the hallway. Nothing turned up.

Pete finally gave up and sat down on his bed in defeat. "I know you're upset, but you have an extra guitar to practice on. I don't have another camera," Alyce complained.

"How am I supposed to duplicate all of my sketches that I did?" Lily asked.

They all began to bicker back and forth, when they heard Pete's aunt calling them down to dinner. They stopped fighting and exchanged glances of confusion. "Why are we being called for dinner? We have been gone for six days!" Alyce asked.

"Dinner? Why would anyone be worried about dinner? Why isn't anyone worried about us?" Lily asked.

"Now I know something really weird is going on. This is the first time Lily's not excited about dinner," Pete said seriously.

Lily looked at Pete and stuck out her tongue. Alyce turned and glanced at the clock, "Guys, it's only been a few hours since we first came up to Pete's room. How can that be?" she questioned. "That's impossible," she continued with a puzzled look on her face.

"That would mean it's still Friday. We still have time to practice for the talent show," Pete said.

"It can't still be Friday, considering all the places we traveled to," Lily interjected.

"There's only one way to find out," Pete said, picking up his remote and turning on his tv.

He put on his favorite channel and said, "See," pointing towards the tv. "This is the music competition show I watch every Friday evening."

He turned to Lily and Alyce and said excitedly, "We still have time to practice for the talent show!"

"We can have all of the time in the world, Pete, but all our stuff is gone. Remember?" Lily sadly reminded him.

"This is getting weirder and weirder," Pete said.

He was about to respond when they heard his aunt calling for the second time from downstairs. "Be right there." Pete yelled down to her. He turned to Lily and Alyce and said, "Not a word to anyone about this. Let's just go eat and come right back upstairs. Then we'll figure out what happened and what we're going to do." Pete firmly said to them. The girls agreed, and the three of them walked out of his bedroom and headed downstairs.

They ran into the dining room and sat down. Pete's Aunt Jane followed a moment later carrying a platter of hamburgers and French fries. "I made you guys something quick, so you can get right back to practicing."

"Aunt Jane, how long have we been upstairs practicing?" Pete asked, taking a bite of his burger.

"Oh, I don't know, a couple of hours, a little more?" she responded.

"I guess we lost track of time," Pete said.

"Did you hear us practicing at all?" Alyce asked.

"What's wrong with you guys?" Aunt Jane responded, with a questioning look on her face.

"Have you seen some weirdo magazine around here?" Lily inquired.

"Alright, maybe you guys should take a break after dinner. I think you have too much music on the brain," Pete's aunt said laughing.

They gobbled down their dinner, thanked his aunt, and rushed back up to Pete's bedroom, still disbelieving they had lost all their stuff. Lily ripped a few pages from her science notebook, grabbed a dull pencil from Pete's desk, and sat down on the floor. "Maybe I can try to draw Dreamy." she said as she began to sketch.

"At least I still have my electric guitar," Pete said, grabbing it out from his closet. "But it doesn't help because I lost all of my music," he said slumping down onto his stool.

"Great, at least you have your guitar, Pete. Lily can sketch some of her drawings from memory. What do I have? My camera, along with all my pictures, is gone," Alyce said, walking over and sitting down on Pete's bed.

"Wait a minute. What about your phone?" Lily asked Alyce.

"Oh, yeah," Alyce said. She reached into her back pocket, pulled out her phone, turned it on, and saw that it was dry and fully charged. "How can that be?" she thought to herself, searching through her phone for any photos of their journey. The only pictures she had were of the landscape. There were no photos of any of the new friends they met along the way.

After a few minutes of everyone moping, Alyce jumped up and said, "I know we're all bummed about losing our stuff." She paused, remembering what Chief Neolin had said. She continued, "We can either do our best and put something together and believe in what we create, or our only other choice is to withdraw from the contest," Alyce said, trying to sound as sensible as possible.

Lily agreed and shook her head yes. "There's no way we're going to do that," Pete said sternly. "Let's get to work!" he said encouragingly. And they did for the next two days.

They had just finished going through their piece one last time. "That was great!" Lily squealed and continued,

"Look, it's only 8:30. There is still an hour before the dance is over."

"Yeah, let's go," Alyce said excitedly.

Pete looked at them both and knew it would be pointless to fight, especially after all they had been through, so he agreed that they all deserved a night of fun.

They quickly got ready, and the three of them walked the short distance to their school. They made it in time to get in a dance or two, and they were happy to show their other friends their new dance moves that they learned. Pete even did a few steps, and the others were all impressed. It was exactly what they needed, to let off a little steam after all the work they did. They stayed until the end and walked home together, smiling and laughing.

CHAPTER 24

The Talent Show

IT WAS TUESDAY BEFORE THEY KNEW IT, AND IT WAS TIME FOR the show. They anxiously awaited back stage for their turn. Their performance went off without a hitch. Pete's music tied in perfectly with Alyce and Lily's part. They walked off the stage, joined the other contestants, and waited for the remaining acts to finish. Pete nervously wiped the sweat from his brow, as Mr. Ashton announced the top three finalists in the show. He looked nervously at Alyce and then at Lily. Alyce offered a small smile, and Lily squeezed his hand. Pete looked over at the other two finalists, as Mr. Ashton announced third place winners, "Charlotte Summers and her brother Charlie." They ran up on stage and got their gift cards.

Pete was growing more anxious by the minute. "Come on, hurry up!" he muttered under his breath. This was it. Pete sat nervously on the edge of his seat, as Mr. Ashton announced the runner up "And second prize goes to Larry Lewis and his one- man band." Pete, Alyce and Lily just sat there for a second, before they realized they had won. Pete jumped up and pulled Alyce and Lily along with him onto the stage to receive their prize, which was a $50.00 gift card and a big, shiny trophy. Pete held the trophy proudly, as someone in the crowd asked them to pose for a group picture. "We did it! We really did it!" Pete said, as he grinned from ear to ear.

Everyone cheered and congratulated them. As they left the auditorium, they felt great! They were so proud that they were able to create the winning piece against all odds. They chatted with friends for a few minutes about their summer plans before starting to walk the few blocks home.

Alyce and Lily couldn't believe they had actually won, and they were so proud of themselves. "I knew we had it in the bag the whole time," Pete bragged.

"Yeah, ok, Pete, you were sweating in there because it was hot, right?" Lily teased.

"Whatever, Lily, we won. That's all that matters," Pete said as he crossed his lawn and saw a huge box on his front porch.

CHAPTER 25
Special Delivery

"WHAT DID YOU ORDER NOW, PETE?" ALYCE ASKED AND rolled her eyes at Lily.

"I didn't order anything," Pete said cautiously, as he looked at the package and noticed it was addressed to him.

There was no return address, and the box was a little beat up looking. There were strange markings, but no stamps. "Hmm, that's interesting," Alyce said, as she offered to help him lug it up to his room.

"What do you think it is?" asked Lily excitedly.

"I have no idea," Pete answered.

They carried the box upstairs and put it down in the middle of Pete's room. He used his scissors from his desk to cut the box open carefully. The three friends stood around anxiously, wondering what it could be. Pete pulled the box flaps open and said, "I must be dreaming," as he pulled his guitar out. The girls stared in awe.

"How can that be?" Alyce asked in disbelief.

"What else is in there?" Lily shouted, jumping up and down.

"See for yourselves," Pete said, as he examined his guitar, and he stepped out of their way.

It was perfect, not a scratch on it. The string that Song's grandma fixed was still in working order.

Alyce screamed happily when she saw her camera in the box. It, too, was in perfect condition. She quickly looked at the pictures on the camera and began to cry happy tears! All her pictures were there.

Lily nudged Alyce out of the way and reached into the box, too. There was her backpack, filled with all her sketches. She hugged it, smiled and said, "I knew you'd make it back to me."

The friends all looked at each other and jumped around, holding hands. It was a miracle! "How did this happen?" Lily shouted.

"How did our stuff make it back?" Pete asked.

"It had to be the Chief," Alyce said calmly. "There is no other explanation."

"Whatever," Pete said. "My baby is back."

Alyce knew how he felt. She was thrilled to have her camera back. Lily just spun around, holding her backpack. They were all thrilled to see their stuff returned unharmed. Alyce and Lily were anxious to go home to examine all of their returned belongings to make sure it was all there. They said good bye to Pete after agreeing that he could keep the trophy at his house. "See you tomorrow," he shouted, as the girls were walking down the stairs.

"Later, Pete," Alyce said.

"I'm a little tired of hanging out with you. I need a break," Lily said.

"No kidding," Pete said.

As the girls bounded down the stairs and out of the house, Pete took one last glance in the box and shouted, "This thing!" He picked up the magazine and tossed it out the opened window next to his bed, just as the girls were passing beneath it. It landed right at Alyce's feet, with the back cover facing up. She bent down, picked it up, and saw that there was a picture of The Great Pyramids of Egypt on it. Alyce looked at Lily, and they both looked up, as Pete stuck his head out the window yelling, "Don't touch that thing!"

"Too late," Lily said, looking up at Pete with a smirk.

The End

THE WEIRDNESS OF WILLOW STREET

BOOK 2
The History Project

CHAPTER 1

School Bells

Lily, Pete, and Alyce walked down Willow Street and headed in the direction of Adams Middle School. It didn't seem possible that the summer was over already. The three friends hadn't had much time to spend together over their break, with them all being so busy. They barely had time to even talk for more than a few minutes. "The Episode" that occurred at the end of the school year with the Talent Show was off limits as far as conversation goes.

Alyce had tried to bring up the subject a few times, and she was always hushed away. Pete would use the excuse that he was getting ready to go to music camp, and he needed to have a clear head to be able to perform well.

Alyce recalled that last night at Pete's, while he was packing to go to camp. Alyce had asked Pete if they could talk about what had happened, and he stubbornly shook his head, "No."

"But that's six weeks away, Pete," Alyce complained. "We need to talk about it now," she insisted, stomping her foot on the floor.

"This time I'm with Pete. I really don't feel like reliving "The Unexpected Vacation Episode" right now, either, Alyce," Lily said firmly, hopping onto his bed.

"We'll discuss it when I get back!" Pete growled, looking at them, "and don't you two go around causing any trouble while I'm away. I'll come back, and the two of you will have taken a trip to the moon!" He hesitated for a moment, and continued, "Remember, we promised not to discuss this with anyone. We don't need everyone thinking we're nuts."

"Alright, alright," Alyce said with a sigh.

"I'll make sure Alyce keeps quiet!" Lily yelled out.

"Terrific! Now I have all the confidence in the world. I'm sure Mr. Mason will know about it, before I even get to camp," Pete said, as he checked around his room one last time to make sure he didn't forget anything.

When Pete returned from camp, he planned on giving free guitar lessons at the youth center a few days a week.

"Ok, seriously, guys, what are you going to be doing while I'm away?" Pete asked them both.

Lily explained that she had volunteered to run the Arts and Crafts Class at the town day camp every morning and that she would be interning at a local art gallery in the afternoons. She was also going to be spending a few weeks with her dad. With so many commitments, Lily would barely have time to see anyone all summer.

Alyce's parents rented an RV for a few weeks and would be taking the family across country to see the Grand Canyon. She was looking forward to all the new sights, but she was even more excited to try out the new camera lens she had finally saved up enough money to buy. She hoped to get a good photo to enter in the photography show at the local junior college.

It was getting late, so Pete patted Lily on her head and promised to text and send them some video music clips that he would be working on at camp. They gave him a quick hug and bounded down his front stairs. They waved one last time, as they crossed the street. They actually all had summer plans, so they wouldn't have much time to spend together anyway.

Lily and Alyce walked up the street in silence for a moment. Lily could sense Alyce's disappointment. She grabbed her hand and softly said, "I'll talk about it with you, Alyce. Don't worry. I won't tell Pete."

"Thanks, Lils, but maybe he's right. Maybe we should talk about this when we all get back from our summer plans," she replied and squeezed Lily's hand in appreciation. "It will go quickly," Alyce thought to herself. "We'll all be so busy that the six weeks will fly by," she hoped.

Just then, Alyce was jolted out of her recollection of that night by Pete, snapping his fingers in front of her face, asking, "Hello, Alyce? Is anybody home?"

Startled, Alyce looked at Pete and then looked up to see that they were standing in front of their school. He smiled at her, and Lily grabbed Alyce's hand. They climbed the steps, and with a little more confidence, they entered through the main doors. They were seventh graders, after all.

They quickly compared their schedules and saw that they were all in History, Lunch, and Math together.

"Ugh! I have Science first period with Mr. Masters!" Lily said, slapping her head. "I've heard that he makes you put frogs to sleep and look at their veins and stuff. Yuck!" she complained.

"Oh, that's just a rumor, Lily!" Pete exclaimed, winking at Alyce.

Alyce stifled a laugh and began heading towards their lockers, with Lily and Pete, following behind her. They talked for another minute before the bell rang, and then they went their separate ways to their first class.

"See you guys in History," Lily yelled, as she got swept up in the sea of students, heading toward the science wing.

Pete and Alyce joined a few of their other friends, who had gathered in the hall, and they all headed towards their first classes. Pete went down the stairs that led to the locker room for gym class, while Alyce made her way up to her English class on the second floor.

CHAPTER 2

The Project

BEFORE THEY KNEW IT, IT WAS THIRD PERIOD, AND LILY HAD reached their History classroom first. She immediately went inside to find three seats together and then went back out into the hall to wait for Pete and Alyce. As soon as she saw them, she ran over, grabbed their hands, and began leading them to their classroom. "I saved us three seats together," she said excitedly, with a big smile on her face. Lily was sitting in front of Pete, and Alyce was across from him in the next row. "That's the best I could do," she said, motioning to the seating arrangement. They both just rolled their eyes and slid into their seats.

The students began to settle down, once the second bell rang, and Pete leaned over to the girls and whispered, "This class should be a breeze. Everyone says Mrs. Hangley barely checks on homework assignments and gives open book quizzes." Pete was about to continue, but stopped mid-sentence, when a tall, attractive woman walked into the classroom. Her brown hair was piled on top of her head, her red glasses were resting on the end of her nose, and she had a pencil stuck behind her ear. She was carrying a huge stack of papers and maps.

"Where's Mrs. Hangley?" Alyce asked in a hushed whisper.

"I have no idea," Pete replied under his breath.

"Maybe she's a substitute?" Lily offered.

"On the first day of school?" Pete asked more to himself than out loud.

The woman placed the stack of books she was carrying on the desk. She cleared her throat, stood up straight, and said, "Good Morning, Class. I know you were all expecting to see Mrs. Hangley, but unfortunately, she had to attend to some family matters, so I will be taking over her classes indefinitely. My name is Ms. Peck," she said, barely cracking a smile. "I don't know how Mrs. Hangley ran her classroom, but I think you will find my methods quite different from what you may have been expecting," she continued. She immediately took roll call and said, "Ok, let's get started."

Pete didn't hear another word she was saying. He was drawing music notes on the cover of his new notebook, counting down the minutes till lunch.

Ms. Peck informed them that their first assignment was going to be a project. Each student would pick a country to research. She walked around the room, amongst the moans and groans of the students, as she explained their assignment in more detail. They would need to complete a model scene and a written report and do an oral presentation. There were even more moans and groans from the students. It was only the first day of school. It was only third period, and they were already being given a huge assignment.

Alyce just sighed and made a few notes in her notebook. Pete was scribbling away, not paying attention at all, and Lily was bouncing up and down in her seat, trying to get Ms. Peck's attention.

"Ok, young lady, you seem very excited for this, so go ahead and pick first," Ms. Peck said, smiling at Lily. Ms. Peck held a small bowl, filled with folded papers inside, in front of her and told Lily to pick one. Lily closed her eyes and stuck her hand into the bowl, mixing the papers around and around. A second later, she pulled out a paper, opened it, and read what was written down.

"Norway! I got Norway!" Lily squealed with delight. "You go next, Alyce," Lily continued excitedly, as the class laughed at her eagerness.

Alyce reached her hand into the bowl and pulled out the very first one that her fingers touched. She unfolded the paper, read it quietly out loud, and said, "India."

"Okay, you are next," Ms. Peck said, turning towards Pete, holding the bowl in front of him.

Pete looked up at Ms. Peck with a confused look. He wasn't quite sure why he was picking a paper out of a bowl, but he went along with it. He reached inside, grabbed one, opened it, and read, "Australia." With a perplexed look on his face, Pete looked around the class and then at Alyce.

After everyone had chosen a country, Ms. Peck went on to explain that they had two weeks to complete their project. "Project? What project?" Pete thought to himself. He knew he had been daydreaming for a minute or two, but "how did he miss this whole 'project' thing?" he thought, looking around in a state of total confusion. His classmates were all taking notes and scribbling things in their notebooks, as fast as they could, but Pete had no idea what was going on.

Ms. Peck returned to the front of the classroom and sat down at her desk. She allowed the students to talk amongst themselves for the last few minutes of class. She noticed that there were a few countries remaining and quickly asked anyone who wanted extra credit to please stay after class for a moment to get their assignment. Just then the bell rang, and the students sprang to their feet and headed for the door. Alyce and Pete gathered their books and made their way to the door as well. Lily stopped at Ms. Peck's desk and shouted, "I'll meet you in the lunchroom." Alyce and Pete waved and filed out of the classroom with the rest of the students.

CHAPTER 3
Lunch Break

ALYCE EXPLAINED THEIR ASSIGNMENT TO PETE, AS THEY MADE their way down the hall to the lunchroom.

"That seems like an awful lot of work for a first day assignment," Pete grumbled, as they picked up their trays and got their lunch.

"Well, we do have two weeks, Pete," Alyce said, as they headed to their usual table and sat down.

"Yeah, I guess that's not too bad," Pete said, "and besides, no offense, Alyce, I'm actually glad we have to work on our own projects. After the talent show chaos last year, I think its best."

Alyce giggled and was about to respond, when Lily came running over to their table. She stood there for a moment, trying to catch her breath, and Pete and Alyce just looked at her, waiting for her to speak.

"Okay. Are you ready for the super coolest thing?" Lily asked, grinning from ear to ear.

"What is it, Lily?" Alyce urged, grabbing Lily's arm and shaking it a little.

"Come on, Lily, what is it? It must be pretty good, if you're making such a big deal about it," Pete said, actually getting a little excited himself by the big smile on Lily's face.

"Okay, okay," Lily said with a mischievous smile on her face. "I signed up for an extra credit assignment in History. I figured I'd get the extra credit in the beginning, as a little cushion for the rest of the year." she continued, still smiling.

"That's what this is all about?" Pete asked. "Some stupid, extra credit project in History?" Pete just shook his head and started reading over some of his music sheets.

"Really, Lily? I thought you had some juicy gossip or something," Alyce said, sounding disappointed.

"Come on, guys, I didn't tell you the best part yet," Lily said. Alyce and Pete both looked at Lily suspiciously, as she continued, "I signed you guys up, too, and Ms. Peck is going to let us work on it as a group extra credit. It took me a couple of minutes to convince her, but I told her how well we worked together last year and how we won the talent show, so I figured what a great way to start the year by working on a project together." By the time she finished, she was out of breath again. Pete and Alyce just stared at her for a minute, with their mouths open. "And wait till you see what we got," she continued, unfazed by their expressions. She opened her fist, and a crumpled, white paper fell onto the table. The three friends looked at it and saw that it read "Egypt".

"This should be fun," Lily said excitedly, looking at Alyce and Pete.

"Oh, great, can't wait to get started," Pete grumbled under his breath.

Alyce glanced at the paper and thought, "Egypt? Coincidence? Or not?"